NEXT OF KIN

ALSO BY SCOTT BARRON

The Forgotten Cross

NEXT OF KIN

SCOTT BARRON

About the author

Scott Barron is a former Royal Marine Commando, trained in arctic, jungle and desert warfare and a veteran of active service in Northern Iraq, Southern Turkey, Northern Ireland and Kosovo.

First published in the UK, 2020

www.scottbarronfiction.com

A CIP catalogue record for this book
is available from the British Library

Paperback ISBN: 978-1-5272-5550-0

For Victoria and Saskia

Prologue

Like most people who have been murdered, I knew my killer. I didn't die by a random act of violence, committed by a stranger, in fact, I knew them very well.

The room was almost entirely dark. The light from the screen of the life support machine keeping the man alive, bathed the area in a dull green gloom. The machine monitored the rhythm of his heart and the amount of drugs that were being pumped into his bloodstream. The ventilator hissed and clicked as it rose and fell, forcing oxygen into his lungs. He had been stripped naked and wrapped in a threadbare sheet pulled tight around his body. His ribs stuck out through the translucent fabric as his chest kept pace with the ventilator.

The thin tube of a saline drip snaked around its stand, its sharp tip invading his body via a vein on the back of his hand. The skin around it was sore and bruised as if it had been inserted with no regard for comfort. Above the bed, there was no name for the patient, just the number 49 written on an old dirty whiteboard.

The door opened inch by inch, revealing a silhouetted figure wearing a white doctors coat. Taking a few paces into the room he stood still, peering into the darkness until his eyes grew used to the light. He covered his nose as he walked over to the bed, the musty, dirty smell offensive to him.

He leaned in close to study his patient's face, searching for any signs that he knew he was there; there were none. The doctor pulled on a latex glove and gripped the man's throat feeling for the bulge of the intubation tube inside his windpipe. The ventilator fought to inflate the man's chest, so he squeezed harder until the screen on the life support machine changed to display a steady flatline.

He let go and laughed loudly before spitting onto the man's face, watching it drip through the stubble on his cheek to soak into the grimy pillow.

Then he turned and left the room not bothering to close the door behind him.

Scott Barron

PART ONE

BLOOD & DUST & RUIN

CHAPTER ONE

Food of love

Kani Masi - Northern Iraq, mid-1980s.

Kani Masi is a small settlement in the base of a valley hemmed in by steep snow topped ridges. Despite bordering on Syria and Iran, the people living there have always considered themselves to be Kurdish. The valley follows the shape of the Diyala River; its source beginning somewhere between the taller of the two peaks dominating the North. Due to the steep mountains to the north, the only way to reach Kani Masi was via a rugged trail to the south which was at least two days walk away. Many of the original settlers had grown tired of living in such a remote area and had left to seek a modern way of life in the Kurdish capital city of Erbil. Of those who stayed, there was a real sense of community and the remaining families would often travel great distances to trade and to allow their children to play.

Alaz, a tall, slim man with dark brown skin and friendly brown eyes owned a settlement in the valley. He had never known his mother who had died in childbirth, and his father, a leading member of the local PKK rebels, was killed in an ambush near to the Turkish border when Alaz was only nineteen years old. Since he had no brothers or sisters, Alaz had inherited the farm which was situated about half a days walk away from the river. Despite the unrelenting heat, Alaz had always been able to grow a reasonable range of crops in the parched, sandy ground. Over the years he had accumulated a small herd of goats, several hens and a donkey that was particularly fond of braying loudly at night for no reason in particular.

Alaz rested his palms on the rough wooden gate to his field and closed his eyes, savouring the slight breeze flowing down from the northern end of the valley. He swept his long black hair from his damp forehead, opened his eyes and looked down at the gate to see a fly starting its careful approach towards him. It paused to rub its legs together, in the way that flies do, before taking off in a zig-zagging flight towards the donkey. With his attention on the fly, Alaz hadn't heard her approach and was pleasantly surprised when he felt her arms encircle his waist as she planted a sweet kiss on the side of his neck. Turning to look at his wife Amira he paused; he was entranced by her eyes — he still thought they were the most beautiful things he had ever seen.

'What are you thinking my love?' She asked.

He smiled and took hold of her small delicate hands, they felt warm and soft, 'about when we first met at the

gathering to celebrate the new year. Do you remember?'
Alaz said.

Amira nodded as she unfolded his hands and smoothed
her fingers over his calloused palms.

'You work too hard,' she said softly.

'I didn't want to go to the feast, but my mother forced
me to go,' he continued.

'Yes, I still remember the sweet smell of the nan
breads and the lamb seasoned with meadow herbs, it was
so nice. And the food you tried to steal from me of
course,' she teased.

In fact, it was hunger that had brought them together,
as they had both reached out for the same piece of bread
at the same time. The food had smelled so good, and
Alaz was so hungry after a full day working on the farm
that he couldn't wait to devour it. When he glanced up to
look at who was trying to take his food away from him,
he couldn't help but gawk at the girl who had hold of the
other end of the bread. Not wanting to give it up, he kept
hold of the bread; that was until he saw Amira smile at
him. Then he forgot about it and stared back at her with
a silly grin on his face. Alaz had never seen anybody so
beautiful, as the fire lit up her face showing off her high
cheekbones and her big brown eyes.

Amira broke the bread in half and offered it to Alaz
who accepted it and stuttered out an awkward thank you.
She smiled at him again, and Alaz knew then that he was
in love. That night they stole away to sit on a nearby hill
to watch the families below, dance and share their food
and drink. Alaz studied Amira's face as she watched the
elders break home-made pots for good luck, loving the
way the stars twinkled in her eyes.

As the first batch of fireworks exploded high in the cloudless sky, he nervously reached out for her hand. Amira rested her head against his shoulder and squeezed his hand tenderly. And as they held hands for the first time, there was no other place in the world they wanted to be.

They married the following year on her 18th birthday. Amira looked sensational in her blue silk dress and matching shoes her mother had bought for her. She complimented the dress with gold bracelets and earrings that sparkled when the sun caught them. Dressing up was lovely of course, but all Amira longed for was to be alone with Alaz. She thought that he looked magnificent in his bright white robes and she loved how he had styled his beard, making him look much older.

Amira's parents had travelled in from the capital and insisted on the Kurdish custom of having a public procession after the wedding to Alaz's farm. It was lovely hearing the kind words that the families said about them as they walked, but the journey seemed to take an age, and it was already getting dark. When they finally reached Alaz's farm, Amira's mother began to weep, perhaps realising that she was losing her daughter tonight.

The celebrations paused as Amira went inside with her mother, as was tradition, Alaz remained outside until his new bride was ready to welcome him in when the festivities had finished. It was the first time that Amira had been into his house and she gingerly stepped over the threshold and paused to look back at Alaz, her soon to be husband. Alaz thought she was smiling at him, but he wasn't sure as he couldn't see through the lace veil covering her beautiful face. Kurdish custom dictated that new brides had to sit alone inside the house for two hours while the guests dined and danced outside. The two hours symbolised their two separate lives and, when the feast finished, Alaz would go into the house, and they would be united as a married couple.

Amira stood in the central living area, which was pleasantly lit by candles, listening to the cheerful sounds of the celebration held in her honour. A fire smouldered in the wide fireplace, and she watched its flames twirl and dance as if trying to match the music outside. A faint stale smell that she couldn't quite place lingered in the room, but the scents from the bunches of wild Iris's and Damask roses did their best to mask it. A gentle breeze blew smoke back down the chimney, the smell of the flowers mixed with it to create a pleasing aroma. Amira took a large candle from the mantlepiece and sauntered around the room, using it to examine the once colourful tapestries on the walls. The widest of them, holding pride of place in the room, showed a tale of nameless men on horseback, curved swords held aloft fighting in a once important, but now long forgotten battle. Amira touched the coarse woven fabric.

It would definitely have to go she thought. The uneven stone floor was hidden under a patchwork of thick rugs and pieces of carpet. In one corner of the room behind an assortment of cushions, she saw Alaz's AK47 rifle leaning against the wall. Amira had never seen one up close, and she was at once attracted to the weapon. She held the candle near to it, looking at the nicks and scrapes in the wooden stock and the sleek barrel telling its own story of past battles. Amira wondered if it had been used to kill, if somebody had followed another person through the sights and pulled the trigger, ending a life. She crouched down and reached out to touch the hard wooden handle, letting her fingers trace the curve of the trigger, but when she felt the safety catch, hot wax spilled from the candle burning her hand. Amira blew onto her hand as she placed the candle back on the mantlepiece then made herself comfortable on the cushions, picking at the wax as it hardened.

The celebrations seemed to take forever to finish, and she jumped in shock when two volleys of AK47 fire signalled the end. She could hear the low murmurs and loud, knowing laughs of the men as they wished Alaz luck, and she thought she heard her mother crying again. Alaz waited patiently until everybody had left his compound before he made his way back to his house, no it was no longer his house – it was now their home. The wind was picking up now, the cloudless sky had already sapped the ground of the heat it held onto in the daytime. As he walked, Alaz's eyes were drawn to the sky, and he paused to watch a falling star trace a bright path high in the heavens above. With no lights in the valley, the sky sparkled like a vast tapestry painted with billions of stars. He strolled along, tracing the patterns of the constellations and as he got closer to the house, he saw a ribbon of grey smoke trickling out of the chimney, like a smoke signal urging him to hurry home. Alaz found himself standing outside their house, looking at candlelight escaping through a gap at the bottom of the door where he hadn't cut it evenly.

He could still hear singing as the families made their way back down the valley and he stared at the door handle listening to their voices gradually fading away. Suddenly feeling very nervous, he smoothed down his robes and took a deep breath as he reached for the door handle, but before he touched it, Amira flung the door open to meet him.

'Finally!' she said, 'I thought it would never end!'

'Me too!' replied Alaz, looking at his beautiful wife. He looked into her eyes through the veil, but they were unreadable. She led him into the house and turned to look at him. He didn't know what to say to her or what to do; it was like they had only just met.

It was Amira who broke the silence.

'Alaz.'

'What?'

'My veil, you need to lift it from my face, otherwise it is very bad luck for the future.'

'Oh… yes, of course,' he said, taking hold of the bottom of it, embarrassed that his hands were shaking. Amira smiled at her husband as he gently lifted the veil from her face and started to fold it into a neat square.

'Come,' she said, taking his hand and leading him towards their bedroom. Alaz forgot all about folding the veil as it fell from his hands to the floor, and when he looked at Amira, this time there was no doubt what the look in her eyes meant.

It was the perfect end to a perfect day, yet soon they would both be dead.

CHAPTER TWO

Watch and Shoot, Watch and Shoot

Alaz's and Amira's Farm - Kani Masi, early 1990's.

The peace that had surrounded Alaz shattered as he was awakened from his deep sleep by the delightful sound of laughter coming from outside. He reached out for Amira, but her side of the bed was cold and empty, and it took him a moment to remember she'd spent the night at their friend's house. Alaz shuffled across to her side of the bed and listened to the noises of his children playing while he scraped at the melted wax on the bedside table that was once last nights candle. Alaz walked to the window, yawning as he wiped the sleep from his eyes before looking for the source of the noise. He watched his children kicking up clouds of dust; their hands linked in a contest of strength which seemed to end in a draw when they both tumbled to the ground in fits of laughter.

Growing bored with wrestling, his boys, Salim and Goran, turned their attention to capturing one of the chickens, which was getting the better of both of them.

'You two never learn,' said Alaz, smiling, causing wrinkles to appear next to his eyes.

'Watch, papa watch!' Shouted Goran, as he circled behind the chicken which seemed to be losing interest in their game. With Goran holding its attention Salim lunged at it, but the chicken saw its chance and escaped through the fence into the goat pen.

'Salim you fool, I nearly had it then!' Exclaimed Goran as he watched a brown and white feather drift to the ground in a lazy circle. The donkey looked up, unamused from the other side of the fence.

At six years old, Goran was two years younger than his brother Salim, but he had a sturdy build which came in handy during their frequent play fights. They both had their mother's eyes which Alaz was grateful for, he thought his wife's Amira's eyes were the most beautiful things he had ever seen, more beautiful than the brightest star in the night sky.

'Right then, looks like I will have to capture you now,' teased Goran as he took up a low stance with outstretched arms. Salim was ready for the challenge, matching his brother's actions, as they pursued each other around in circles. Alaz sat on the bed to get dressed then made his way out to the courtyard and wandered over to where the children were playing, a small plume of fine powder rising with each footstep.

Despite being early, the sky was clear of clouds, and Alaz knew it would be sweltering today. Although there was a slight breeze, it was providing no real cooling effect and he was glad to be wearing his loose robes, although even these were clinging to his skin in the soaring heat. Beads of sweat formed quickly on his brow, trickling down his face like hot candle wax every time he moved.

'Enough now boys! You know your mother disapproves of you fighting,' Alaz said in that tone of voice fathers have which makes their children stop and listen.

He leaned against the faded whitewashed wall of his house and continued, 'your mother left yesterday to visit baby Ayden; he'll be two years old today. What should we do until she comes back?' he asked, as he picked at a flaking piece of wall already knowing what they would say.

'Shoot! Let us shoot your Kalashnikov!' shouted Salim excitedly. The AK47 had once been Alaz's fathers, and it had come to be in his possession through a survivor of a failed mission that his father had been part of. The rifle had come back, but his father had not. Alaz wiped sweat from his eyes with the back of his sleeve.

'I'm not sure your mother would approve; you know she doesn't like you touching it.'

'I know, but she is so far away down the valley, she will not really hear it. And we can say it was you who was firing it anyway.' Salim said with a mischievous glint in his eye.

Alaz sighed, 'okay. Walk out one hundred paces Salim, then gather some rocks to make targets about the size of a man, let's see if you can hit them this time.'

'Can you count that high Salim, all the way to one hundred?' Goran teased.

'Goran, behave yourself. Will you shoot today as well?' Alaz asked, 'you'll have to learn one day you know.'

'No, I'll just watch from our room to see how bad at it he is,' replied Goran as he turned and walked back to the house with his father.

Amira had warned the boys not to touch the rifle, and Goran didn't want to fire it at all after hearing Alaz talking about how his father had died. He had been hit by a mortar shell and not enough of his body could be found to return home to bury. But it occurred to Goran that if this was true, then his AK47 must also have been destroyed, but nobody ever mentioned that. Goran reasoned that if people in the PKK knew you could shoot, then they would take you away and make you fight for them. Even at his young age, Goran knew this wasn't right, but Salim loved shooting, and he regarded the AK47 with a kind of awe.

When they were alone in their room, he would tell Goran stories of how he would find and slay the men who had killed their grandfather. Salim would dance around in the candlelight in front of the big tapestry, the one with the men on horses and curved swords, giving the men names and describing how he would hunt down and avenge their grandfather, shooting them with the AK47.

Salim ambled back after setting out two piles rocks and saw Goran sitting on the window ledge of their room, his feet resting on the ridge that stuck out about a foot lower than the sill.

'Goran move over to Papa's room. You will have a better view of me hitting them all,' Salim shouted up to his brother whilst kicking a scorpion out of the way.

Salim had been stung by one once as he tried to pick one up to chase Goran with it and he was still wary of them. He watched its legs thrashing around until it righted itself and as it walked away, Salim kicked it again, sending it crashing sideways into a rock. Clear liquid seeped from its body as the scorpion crept slowly away, its legs not working properly now and its stinger twitching erratically. Goran quickly hopped over to the other ledge and waved back; it was his favourite trick to avoid being caught when they played hide and seek. He would hide in their room, and if he heard Salim coming, he would move from room to room to avoid getting caught. He was so good at it that sometimes Salim gave up and sulked for a while afterwards.

Alaz came out of the house and passed the AK47 assault rifle to his son and grinned as he watched him struggle with the weight.

'One day soon, you will hold this as if it was as light as a feather,' said Alaz.

'Yes, yes,' Salim replied, as he flattened out the area where he would shoot from with this shoe, muttering something as he shook the dust and small stones from his sandals.

After a final check of the ground for rocks and anything that might sting him, he set himself up in the kneeling position that his father had taught him and looked through the iron sights.

'Need to clean it Father, there is rust on it.'

'Thank you for offering son, now concentrate. Slow your breathing down and take the shot when you feel ready,' Alaz replied.

Salim pulled the hard wooden stock tight into his shoulder, lining up the rear sight with the front one on top of the muzzle. Once he'd done that, Salim focused solely on the front sight and allowed the rear one to become blurred. All was silent except for the occasional cluck from the chickens or the bleating of the goats. He squinted as the sunlight reflected on the dull metal barrel then concentrated on his breathing, the rifle rising and falling as he breathed in and out. He waited for the respiratory pause which naturally happens, as he knew this was when the rifle would be at its stillest. Sweat stung his eyes making Salim snatch at the trigger, his shoulder jerking backwards as it absorbed the weapons recoil like a hard punch. He heard laughter as the bullet missed its target and disappeared far into the distance. Frustrated he repeated the process making sure he squeezed gently on the trigger instead of snatching at it. This time the bullet struck its target and smashed into the pile of rocks sending them flying violently off in all directions.

Alaz patted him on the back and said, 'good — do it again,' then with a sad sigh he added, 'and keep doing it until you don't miss any at all.'

CHAPTER THREE

11

By the sixth day God saw all that he had made, and it was very good. And there was evening, and there was morning, but before this, the earth was formless and empty and dark, so very dark.

Then God said, "let us make mankind in our image."

But somewhere amongst all this wonderful creation, He forgot to take away the darkness and the only place it could go was into the heart of man.

CHAPTER FOUR

Empty Envelopes

The downwash from the CH-53D Sea Stallion flattened the grass into a wide circle as it touched down in the centre of the field in Northern Iraq. The helicopter pilot had flown fast and low, hugging the natural contours of the terrain to evade detection by radar. They had landed just off the border of Turkey, exactly ten miles away from their target. The noise of the rotors was deafening, Grant Ward, the patrol commander, had to resort to using hand signals to direct his team as they unloaded their equipment. Although the intelligence briefing said that there were no enemy in the area, the helicopter door gunner made steady, confident sweeps of the field with his ceiling suspended mini-gun. If anyone surprised them, they would quickly regret it as they found themselves on the wrong end of a thousand .50 calibre bullets per minute. The door gunner tapped the side of his trigger. He was hoping for his first taste of the kill, completely unaware that he would have nightmares about it for the rest of his life.

The first team member out of the helicopter was a tall, well-built black man called Thomas Stone. After years playing quarterback in college, he weighed a solid 250 pounds, his physique and strength earning him the nickname of Rocky. Rocky hauled the heavy rucksacks from the helicopter, dumping them in a pile while his teammates, James Fox and Mark Reid lay on the cold ground scanning the area through the night vision sights mounted on their rifles. It was hard to see over the knee-high grass, but the unmistakable outline of anybody walking around would be clear on the flat open plain. Once all of the equipment was unloaded, the helicopter lifted off straight up into the air before turning south and disappearing into the distance, the whole process of landing and unloading taking less than a minute. When the steady thud of the rotor blades gradually died away, the silence was deafening, and the soldiers lay still in their defensive positions under a night sky that held a thin splatter of clouds. The stink of aviation fuel hung in the air until it was swept away by the breeze and when it finally dissipated, the air tasted clean and fresh.

All the soldiers had encountered fierce fighting in the US invasion of Panama where they had been one of the first SEAL teams to deploy to the country. They had been re-assigned as a special forces team with the call sign of November Three Four, two months ago, becoming the standby unit for any special forces tasks in the Middle East. Although in command of the team, Grant had become a SEAL two years after Rocky and was on the same cohort as James, in fact they almost had the same service number, they were identical except for the final digit. Grant had shown an aptitude for leadership, and he quickly gained a reputation as an adept tactician allowing him to swiftly move up the ranks well ahead of his peers. Although they wore no insignia of rank in case they were captured, Grant was a Lieutenant, Rocky was a Sergeant and both James and Mark were Lance Corporals.

Barely six hours had passed since the order had reached Grant at their forward mounting base on the airstrip at Incirlik in Turkey. At the time, Rocky had been putting James through his paces in a tough deadlift and heavy tyre drag PT circuit while Mark had been perched on the arm of a dusty old sofa killing Nazi zombies on an old PlayStation when Grant excitedly came back with the message that they were to deploy.

'Get it written,' Grant said to Rocky.

Rocky leaned back against the smooth concrete surface of the thick blast wall and looked up at him.

He said, 'you know I ain't got no-one to write to BB,' with a hint of a Texan drawl and a fake sad expression on his face. BB was Grant Ward's unofficial nickname of Bad Bastard because of his volatile temper; which normally surfaced when he was drunk. Grant's volatility was well known throughout the SEAL community, however recently, less and less alcohol was needed to trigger his anger. Rocky had seen him nearly kill James by dry-drowning him during an escape and evasion exercise when the enhanced interrogation phase got out of hand. Being held upside down with a sack over your head while having water poured over your face can break most men; which is why it has been so effective in US black sites all over the world. The technique is designed to simulate the sensation of drowning; after only a few seconds a terrifying need to breath air in through the wet sack becomes overwhelming - any longer than that, the gag reflex kicks in followed by sheer unadulterated terror. After that, any classified mission intelligence can't flow out of the persons mouth fast enough, as they hope to avoid the water again. But they do. Whatever they reveal is confirmed by repeated drownings to check for inconsistencies in their story, which either holds up to scrutiny - or they die by going under too many times.

It was only intended to be a demonstration of how they might be interrogated if caught behind enemy lines, but the incident had unnerved James so much that he handed in an application to move teams. Needless to say, this didn't go down well with Grant who took it as a criticism of his professionalism. Rocky was the only one who dared to call Grant, BB, not because of his own physical presence, but because he had seen Grant use his rage in combat to save soldiers' lives.

When the invasion of Panama had stalled due to sniper fire coming from the Marriott hotel, Grant became frustrated with the lack of air support and had run straight down the street into the hotel to find and kill the sniper. To the amazement of everybody, he hadn't even bothered to zig-zag to make himself a harder target. When asked about it afterwards, he smirked, announcing that he thought the sniper's aim was terrible and he wouldn't be able to reload quick enough to shoot him anyway. The follow-up teams later entered the hotel and discovered the sniper; his face an unrecognisable mess of splintered bone and cartilage. It immediately spread that Grant had wounded the sniper and then sadistically caved his face in with the stock of the sniper rifle. Grant didn't admit doing it, but then again, he didn't deny it either. There were rumours of an official investigation, as under the Geneva Convention even wounded enemy soldiers should receive medical treatment, but as there were no witnesses, the case quickly collapsed. Rather than damaging his reputation, the incident raised Grant's profile, and in the following years, he had his pick of operations to choose from.

'Just write to your mom then Rocky. Or to one of your steroid suppliers,' Grant said, before ordering the rest of the team to write their own letters.

It is a somewhat of an unofficial tradition that all soldiers write a letter to their loved ones in case the mission goes wrong and they never make it back alive. These letters are sealed and stored in the headquarters for the soldiers to collect and destroy once they come back safely. The letters are sacred, and if a soldier does not return, they are sent directly to an officer who turns up on the family's doorstep to literally deliver the bad news.

'You've got ten minutes to finish off your letters, ladies — remember no location specifics. Then I require you all in the ops tent for the full mission briefing,' Grant said.

He looked around at his team. Rocky was chewing his bottom lip struggling to come up with something to write and someone to write to, which made Grant smile. Mark had shifted from the arm of the sofa and was sat in the middle of it, his short, stocky frame taking up a lot of space; he was writing quickly, his mouth moving as he read the sentences back to himself. Mark had a young boy who lived with his ex-wife, but he had recently become engaged to his ex-wife's sister and was no doubt making sure that his words did nothing to damage his new relationship.

'Who are you writing to Mark?' Grant asked.

'Mark paused, scratching the stubble on his chin with the chewed lid on the end of his pen, 'it's complicated,' he replied, without looking up.

Turning, Grant caught sight of James sitting on his folding camp bed staring at him over the top of his dogeared writing pad. When Grant looked over at him, he quickly looked away to avoid eye contact.

'Say hello to your wife and kids for me won't you James.'

James rubbed the back of his neck before resting his arm on his head and looking at him.

'Yeah, you too Lt.'

Satisfied that everybody was doing what they had been told to do, although he would expect nothing less, Grant walked away to find a private spot to write his own letter, whistling the American national anthem as he went.

At the ops briefing, they all assumed that it was just going to be a table-top planning exercise; a sort of what would you do; how would you approach this mission type of thing. They had been made to do this before, frequently with limited time to see how they would cope under pressure. Sometimes they planned the missions and were made to deploy to the helicopters to discover how quickly they could do it. The helicopters would usually take off, circle and land at the cost of $20,000 per hour to the taxpayer. They had all believed that what they had been challenged to plan for was entirely hypothetical — but the helicopter had actually landed, and now they were in theatre on an operational footing to carry out the mission they had planned just hours earlier.

The breeze had dropped now, and the cloudless sky proudly displayed its stars, the light from which had taken billions of years to reach the earth. James scanned the sky for familiar formations, but before he found any, he heard Grant quietly give the order to move. As he stood, James looked over to the base of the mountains about ten miles away as he adjusted the straps of his tactical vest making sure that his knife and grenades were accessible. Carrying a heavy rucksack made the straps dig into the shoulders causing your arms to go numb; apart from the pain, which was annoying, it also meant that you wouldn't be able to shoot accurately. James didn't subscribe to all the 'pain is weakness leaving the body,' SEAL bullshit that Grant and Rocky spouted all the time. Perhaps they believed it, but he didn't. Becoming a SEAL had been the ultimate challenge, a chance to prove that he was worthy of being amongst the 1% who completed Basic Underwater Demolitions Training. At the time he'd been attracted by the glamour of being a SEAL; being the absolute best of the best; taking part in covert operations all over the world and providing high-level intelligence to the CIA and other organisations with abbreviated titles. He had enjoyed Panama, that was real, but to James being a SEAL mainly meant freezing your nuts off laying in holes, eating cold rations straight from the packet and shitting in plastic bags.

Grand had ordered them to patrol in a single file due to the threat of mines and improvised explosive devices buried in the area. The rest of the team passed James with Rocky as the point man; also known as the bullet catchers position, usually the first person to get shot. Perhaps Grant had put him at the front on purpose so he could hide behind him in case the enemy surprised them; Rocky's large frame would be the first obvious target they would see. James was to be the Tail-end Charlie. Again. It was his least favourite position in the patrol as he would spend half the time walking backwards making sure their rear was protected, but he thought he was less likely to be shot at first — or to stand on a landmine. Just need to step in the same place as the man before him, and he would be safe. Probably. Of all the ways a soldier could die he'd hate to go that way; to disappear in a pink mist or worse to lose a couple of limbs; and here, hours away from any possible medivac, surviving that would be virtually impossible.

After only a short while, he was already feeling uncomfortable as the weight of the rucksack relentlessly pulled down on his shoulders as he walked. Despite the coldness of the night, he was already sweating, and he knew it would be a long, tough slog to cross the mountains before dawn.

CHAPTER FIVE

Clear Run

'Hello Zero, this is November Three Four,' said Grant into his throat mic. He swore as static crackled loudly over the radio into his earpiece. After a moment that seemed unbearably long, the response he was hoping for came.

'Roger, November Three Four… mission confirmed… be aware British forces are also operating in the area… remain unseen… Zero out.'

'Okay ladies, we're on task now,' Grant said quietly without looking around. 'I'll take the first watch; we'll rotate in one hour.'

The order needed no confirmation from his team. With a well-practised efficiency, the other team members carefully moved into their positions. Two soldiers slowly turned around to face away from their target and scanned the area through their weapon sights. After a short while, one of them unpacked a sleeping bag and crawled awkwardly into it. The other soldier lay close by on the cold rocky ground providing security, his suppressed AR15 assault rifle ready to deal with any unwanted visitors.

The final team member moved to lie next to the Grant, ready to report any details of the activity below. With slow deliberate movements, Grant carefully took out a small laptop from his rucksack and typed a coded message into it. His fingers tapped lightly on the rubber keys impatiently as he awaited a response. Stifling a yawn, the soldier next to him raised his binoculars to watch the target and followed the boys' playful journey around their yard before their father ushered them inside to go to bed.

'Shit, I hope they're sure about this,' James thought with a rising sense of uncertainty.

CHAPTER SIX

10

If you could find out the day you were going to die would you want to know? And what if you had to die on a specific day, would you choose how you would die? Would you prefer it to happen quickly? A bullet to the head? No? Too violent and not pleasant for the person finding you I guess. What about a slower more relaxed way? How about an overdose in a nice warm bath? Yes, maybe that's the way to go. Apparently drowning is a lovely way to die, take the pills and then just drift under the water and fall asleep. Perhaps I'll do that and slit my wrists as well just to make a point. Yes, you've won, but you know what ass-hole? You'll have to clean up after me.

CHAPTER SEVEN

Manna from Heaven

Kani Masi - Northern Iraq.

It was a clear, cold night, and Alaz was enjoying the pleasant summer breeze flowing down from the mountains. He closed his eyes, savouring the silence until the baleful braying of a donkey wandering around somewhere nearby ruined it. It was almost midnight, and his boys were sound asleep after a full day of wrestling and running around the yard. Alaz was keenly awaiting his wife's return after her visit to the family down the valley to celebrate the second birthday of their friend's son Ayden. The moon cast a welcome pale silver light and Alaz could just about see the top of the house at the far end of the valley where his beautiful wife would soon begin to make her way back home from.

'I am a truly fortunate man,' he told himself as he stared up at the sky. Alaz loved looking at the constellations when the nights were clear, and he tried to find the stars of Orion's Belt to join them together into their familiar shape when something caught his eye.

'That's strange - I didn't expect there to be fireworks tonight to celebrate Ayden's birthday — unless Eland has come back already,' he said to himself. Alaz frowned when he realised that the fireworks weren't coming from his friend's house but from somewhere behind the mountains. He rubbed the back of his neck as he watched a cluster of six fireworks — no they weren't fireworks, fireworks go up, and these were coming straight down; the tail end of them burning a dull red colour like the dying embers of a fire.

They were falling towards the house where Amira and the child were. Ten feet from the ground, a miniature parachute deployed from the rear of them, and they landed in a circle around the house, settling with a soft thud, hardly making any noise at all.

As well as Alaz, also watching the parachutes deploy through the light intensifying scope of his rifle, was the patrol commander of the small team of soldiers in the mountains. The patrol commander gestured to the soldier to his left and nodded twice before turning his attention back to the area where the rockets had landed. The soldier to his left opened a small laptop and entered a six-digit authentication code and less than a second later the tips of the rockets split open releasing a faint yellow vapour.

Unsure whether to go to the house or stay here close to his children, Alaz chose the latter. He strained to see the house in the distance illuminated by the pale moonlight, and he saw that the fireworks had only caused a light cloud of dust to rise and that was already settling.

'Nothing to worry about. I'll look at them in the morning,' Alaz said, looking back up to the stars.

Amira sat cross-legged on a plush pile of rugs with the child on her lap. As she looked at him, she was enchanted by the pure, innocent beauty of his big deep brown eyes as he considered her face.

'When will Eland return?' said Amira, as she lifted the boy to kiss his forehead.

'Soon I expect. Eland has nothing to hide,' replied Hana, the baby's mother.

Unofficially the Kurds were still at war with Turkey who had tried to clear the areas where the Kurdish had settled. Groups of armed PKK rebels often mounted fighting patrols against the Turks along the border to show their power in the area.

'I told him they would be okay to travel on their own, but he wouldn't listen,' said Hana.

'Yes, but he wasn't going to let your mother and father travel to the Erbil alone was he.'

'Besides,' Amira continued, 'if your father fell again and broke his other arm could you imagine how much he would complain?'

Hana nodded and smiled.

'Probably got held up on the way back at one of their checkpoints. They keep trying to make him join them you know.' She said.

'Oh, Hana you must not let him, please don't — you know what happened to Alaz's father,' pleaded Amira.

'He won't join, not now we have this little one to care for,' she replied, stroking her son's light brown hair.

The women had finished eating, so Hana cleared away

the heavy earthen-ware plates, and Amira played
peekaboo with the boy much to his delight.

Hana's house was almost identical to Amira's, with a
doorway from the small courtyard leading to the central
living area. In the corner of the living area, the wide
fireplace glowed dark red as the last of the logs burnt
down to ash; the burning wood filled the room with a
pleasantly sweet, smoky smell. The fireplace looked too
big for the room, but it was purposely built that way so
there was enough room to cook in it and dry out clothes
in the winter months. The whitewashed walls were as
smooth as they could be and there were brightly
coloured handmade rugs hanging on the walls. A set of
stone stairs led up from the corner opposite the fireplace
onto a landing, from which there were two equally sized
bedrooms: one room for Hana, Eland and their son and
the other for her parents.

'I better open the bedroom doors to trap the warm air
from the fire,' Hana said, setting the plates down near to
the door so they could be cleaned outside in the
morning.

'Yes, it looks like it will be cold tonight,' Amira
replied, standing up to close the blind to the window in
the living area.

'You know I could teach you how to make curtains for
the rooms like I...' Amira said, but her voice faded, and
she stopped mid-sentence as she saw something through
the window.

'Did you see that?' she said to Hana.

'Hana looked past her through the window, 'yes, what
is it?'

'I bet Alaz and the boys have come over and are

playing tricks on us! Let's go out and catch them at it -
I'll be out with the little one in a minute,' Amira said as
she searched for the blanket she had made as a gift for
his birthday. Amira had enjoyed making it, but it had
taken her an age to get it finished because she had
braided his name around the edges in brightly coloured
wool. Wrapping the infant in his blanket, Amira went
outside and saw Hana kneeling on the ground next to a
narrow, dull grey coloured cylinder. The parachute that
had slowed its descent flapped pathetically in the breeze
like a dying bird trapped in a net; its cords twisted
tightly around the fabric.

'What is it Amira?'

'I don't know, is there any writing on it, any symbols?'

'No. Oh wait, there's some writing here at the end next
to this line going around it,' Hana said, stepping closer
to read the small Arabic symbols printed on the metal
surface of the cylinder.

'Be careful. You don't know what that thing is, or
where it has come from,' warned Amira.

Looking back at her friend, Hana said, 'you worry too
much Amira, but that's why I know you and Alaz will
make great Godparents for Ayden,' before turning her
attention back to the object.

It took a second for Hana's eyes to grow accustomed
to the poor light as she tried to read the symbols on the
side.

'It say's "Halabja 2," on it,' she stuttered when she
realised the meaning behind the words.

'Oh Amira, you don't think they are doing it to us
again…'

The sound of her words petered out as she leaned

closer to the object to reread the symbols, hoping that she had misunderstood them. As she did so, the thin line she had been looking at made a clicking noise, the noise you might make by clicking your fingers, and a pale yellow mist flooded out. It smelt foul and Hana quickly stood up to escape the cloud. She turned to Amira and struggled to say something, but no words would come. She rubbed at her eyes which had suddenly started to itch and water so much that she couldn't see anything. Amira stood frozen in fear as she looked at her friend; the infant cooed contentedly into her shoulder.

Hana shook. Then mucus streamed from her nose, mixing with her tears as it dripped off her face and down over her chest in thick clear strands. She tried speaking again, but all that came was drool that dribbled out over her chin. Clawing at her face and eyes, she suddenly stood still and slowly raised her hand and pointed a crooked finger at Amira.

Then she shuddered violently as if she was being electrocuted, vomit spewing explosively from her mouth towards Amira who was already backing away from her. Hana fell to the ground and crawled towards Amira on her hands and knees like some kind of injured animal. Her bladder and bowels opened at the same time.

Hana's body slumped, and she collapsed to the ground and rolled on to her side, vomit, urine and faeces leaked out of her body and soaked into the ground, ending this woman's life in a most disgusting way.

Amira just stood still looking at Hana until the baby shifted, seeking warmth and snuggling closer to Amira's neck. Without looking away, Amira unwrapped her headscarf with one hand and held it over the baby's mouth. She took one last look at her ruined friend, then she turned and ran.

CHAPTER EIGHT

Choices, Choices

As the clouds slithered past the moon, Alaz could just about make out the shape of a figure moving away from their friend's house in the distance.

'Ah, she can't wait to see me, so she is leaving early.' Alaz glanced back to check that he'd shut the door to the house as he left his compound, pulling the flimsy wooden gate closed behind him.

'I'm sure the boys will be okay - I'll go to meet her halfway,' it's not too far he reasoned, breaking into a slow jog, not wanting to leave them alone for too long.

Amira had only run a short distance when she felt her chest tightening. She realised that her pace was slowing, but no matter how hard she tried to speed up she couldn't. Her shin scraped against the edge of a sharp rock, cutting a deep gash into the skin but she barely noticed it as her legs grew steadily weaker. As she staggered on, Amira stumbled forward only just managing to remain upright with the child still held close to her chest. Her run had slowed to a shuffle now, all she could think about was making it back home. Amira strained to look at her house where her loving husband and beautiful children were sleeping. She knew that if she could reach there, Alaz would protect her and keep the baby safe.

Amira watched the strange shadows cast by the moon spread out over the flat ground then contract like a giant hand closing into a fist. As she stumbled on, Amira thought she might be hallucinating when she saw a figure running towards her. Squinting and blinking hard several times, trying to clear her watering eyes, she thought that it looked like Alaz running towards her. But she couldn't be sure, her eyesight deteriorated with each passing second and it was becoming harder and harder to see.

As she struggled on, Amira knew she was no longer heading towards her home; she was straying away from it somehow in a wide arc, but she couldn't understand why or force herself to change direction. Confused, Amira stopped walking, giving up on trying to gain control of her own body and decided to wait for Alaz to arrive. She tried to stand still but found herself swaying backwards and forwards like a drunk. She couldn't feel her feet. Then she felt the insides of her thighs become wet as first her bladder and then her bowels opened.

'No! Don't come!' She struggled to shout, but it came out as a mere whimper, and she wasn't convinced that she'd actually said the words or just thought them. Exhaustion swept over Amira like a sandstorm, forcing her to sit down awkwardly on the rough sandy ground.

She tried to speak but this made her vomit over her chest and legs. After trying to wipe her mouth with the back of her numb hand, she slowly peeled away the scarf to peek at the boy's face. Ayden looked up at Amira with his big brown eyes, and Amira stared down at him for what seemed like a lifetime. Something was wrong. Ayden didn't blink once in all the time Amira looked at him. He had big beautiful eyes, but there was no life behind them now. Amira wept pathetically, placing him down to the ground as gently as she could, then she slumped forward and started to shake uncontrollably.

Alaz arrived out of breath and couldn't believe what he saw, his beautiful wife rolling around in the dust in agony. He squatted down and pulled her close, holding her head steady in his hands. Tears and mucus streamed down her face over his hands, and when he looked at her, he struggled to hide his fear from her. He didn't know what was happening or how to help her. Alaz felt worthless; his only purpose in life was to look after her and their boys, and he was failing her. Alaz wrapped her in his arms as Amira clung weakly to the shoulder of his robe. He wanted to stay here forever; holding his wife, keeping her safe, making everything all right like he had promised her on their wedding day. Everything was silent except for the noise of her ragged breathing. After a short while, he felt her tug weakly on his shoulder.

'What is it my love?' he said gently. Amira didn't respond straight away, so he asked her again and saw her fight to raise her arm. His eyes moved down her shaking arm, and he saw she was trying to point at their home. Fear rushed through his veins as he turned to see what she was pointing at. Alaz watched the cluster of silent fireworks floating slowly down towards their house. Amira pulled him close; her warm vomit sticking to his cheek and whispered, 'go.'

Alaz froze to the spot with indecision; should he stay, or should he leave? He didn't know what to do. Alaz opened his mouth to speak or scream — but did neither, and when he felt wetness on his cheeks, it took him a moment to realise that he was crying.

'Amira, my love,' he said, as she stroked her damp hair before settling her onto the ground. He placed the small infant on her chest wrapping her arms around his little body to protect him.

'I'll be back soon,' he declared, then he turned and ran faster than he ever thought he could. Sweat and tears stung his eyes making it hard for him to see and he stumbled, falling into a dip in the ground as his legs gave way underneath him. He paused momentarily to catch his breath listening for any noise, but if there was any, he couldn't hear it over the boom of his heart pounding in his chest.

'Calm down. It's no good if I don't get to my boys safely.'

Sitting back on his heels, Alaz rubbed his eyes, cursing as he blinked to clean away the dirt that had got in there from his hands. He heard a soft wheezing noise nearby and looked around bewildered trying to find the source.

'No, no, no...' he said when he realised where it was coming from. He clambered on all fours crawling towards his donkey as it continued making its pathetic, desperate whine as it clung to its last minutes of life.

Alaz lay next to the donkey and stroked the soft fur on its neck, and as he looked into the animal's big kind eyes, he could see the moon reflected in them. The donkey shuddered and exhaled for the last time. Alaz could still see the moon in its eyes, but it was not as bright as it once was, perhaps after tonight, it would never seem as bright again.

Alaz shivered.

'I'm getting cold.'

Alaz suddenly had a peculiar taste in his mouth: it reminded him of lilac flowers or garlic or onions; he couldn't tell which, but it was intoxicating, and as he savoured the sweet, spicy taste, he realised that he had an uncontrollable urge to piss. He wiped his nose on his sleeve and watched a wispy cloud pass in front of the moon. As it cast its pale gloom down on to the ground something glinted on the hillside drawing Alaz's attention to it.

'What is that?'

Alaz rubbed at his eyes and saw the glint again — then it was gone.

'I'm seeing ghosts.'

His wet trousers clung to his legs as he struggled to his feet, he ran again and then he stopped abruptly. Squinting through misty eyes, he stared hard at the shapes on the hillside. They are just rocks or bushes he thought as he stood there absently picking chunks of his wife's vomit from his beard.

Confused, he realised that the shapes had changed and were now moving down the slope towards his house. The soldier at the front raised his rifle to look at Alaz through the light intensifying sight, and for a fleeting moment, his face was illuminated as a pale green mask.

Alaz shivered with fear and ran as if his life depended on it.

Because it did.

CHAPTER NINE

King of Spades

In the build-up to the Gulf war, the United States tried canvassing support from its allies throughout NATO; but the major players such as France, Germany and the United Kingdom were reluctant to commit troops to a war with a questionable justification for it.

Without a substantial representation from NATO, as soon as the United States moved troops over the border, it would be seen as a sovereign state attacking another sovereign nation without United Nations backing. Not that the Americans were against going it alone, far from it as the people of Iran and Panama could testify, but this is illegal in the eyes of the free (and not so free) world, for obvious reasons.

The world powers would not tolerate moves like this, barely one step removed from modern-day colonisation. What was needed was something that would get the United Nations all worked up — and in doing so making it impossible for countries to not dispatch troops to support the United States war effort. Some event or some kind of irrefutable evidence needed to be found and presented to the United Nations.

If evidence could be found that he had used chemical weapons again, the United States would have their pick of countries to choose from.

If it could be proved that Saddam had access to weapons of mass destruction — primed and ready to launch over its the borders into other countries, this would undoubtedly be enough. Anyhow it's not like he hadn't ordered the use of mustard gas in 1988 in the village of Halabja which slaughtered thousands of Kurds. Surely that can be classed as mass destruction, if not genocide.

CHAPTER TEN

Hunters' Moon

Rocky signalled for the team to halt as he aimed at the lunging, stumbling man and they immediately went down on one knee into defensive positions. He raised his rifle aiming for the centre of the man's torso, no need to go for the head, that would just be showing off anyhow. Rocky wanted to drop him and finish him off close up if he hadn't died right away. There was something satisfying about seeing the results of your work up close. He tracked the man's movement, and when his chest lined up in the centre of the crosshairs, he gently squeezed the trigger firing a single shot.

The man crashed down to the ground.

Then a few seconds later he got up and started running again.

'Oh, for fuck's sake Rocky! Do I have to do everything myself!' Grant said, pushing him to one side.

Grant raised his rifle carefully and followed the

running figure. He aimed just in front of the man in line with his knee to take into account the speed he was moving, and the curving trajectory that the bullet would take.

He fired, and this time the shot found its target.

Alaz spun around violently as the bullet struck him in his left shoulder, smashing into his collar bone, taking skin and bone fragments with it through his lung and out of his body.

The silenced AR15 assault rifles had made no noise, Alaz was unaware he was being shot at. Moments before, he had been running too fast and had stumbled into a dip in the ground - when he stood up to set off again, he had been shot.

The bullet smashed into Alaz like a sledgehammer, the impact spinning him around twice until he ended up on his back, the centre of his spine resting painfully on the top of a small pointed rock that cut into his skin.

Alaz screamed in agony, or at least he thought he did, he wasn't sure. He lay sprawled on the ground unable to move, gasping for air, sweat stinging his eyes, and there was that smell. The stench was disgusting. It took him a few moments to realise that he had soiled himself.

He searched for the stars of Orion's Belt in the sky, and just as he started to join them up, he passed out and was immersed in a colourless dream full of horror that seemed to last for an eternity. Something woke him. It was the angry cry of a donkey somewhere in the distance. The noise saddened him as he thought of his donkey, the one he had raised from a foal, the one that his boys had ridden on as young children, the one that had been a faithful, hardworking servant for many years, the one that was no longer alive.

His boys! He had to get to his boys.

Alaz coughed, and the pain was incredible, like nothing he had ever experienced, a sharp excruciating pain like the sting of a thousand scorpions which became worse with each breath. Alaz tasted blood in his mouth and tried to spit it out but swallowed most of it.

He slipped in and out of consciousness. He dreamed of his boys when they were beautiful young babies and then saw them as grown men — powerfully built and handsome. He dreamt of his Amira from the first time they had met as they argued over the bread at the celebration, the dream was a joyful one which seemed to last forever, and he didn't want it to end. Alaz woke again, and he saw the moon directly above him. It was the brightest it had ever been, and when he lapsed back into his dreams, this was all he saw; the moon bright and sharp and pure in the heavens.

When he awoke again, he was confused as the moon was no longer there, something had taken its place, but he couldn't make out what it was.

When Alaz eventually managed to focus, he saw a camouflaged face looking down at him. He clawed at the sandy ground in terror cutting the ends of his fingers on sharp rocks and tried to scream a warning to his boys. But before he could, the muzzle of the rifle was thrust into his mouth splitting his lips and sending smashed teeth down his throat.

Alaz felt the intense heat from the muzzle flash for a split second; then everything exploded into a burst of intense white light.

This time there were no dreams.

There was nothing, not even darkness.

CHAPTER ELEVEN

Twice Dead

The smell of cordite, charred flesh and blood hung heavy in the air. James screwed his nose up in disgust at what he'd just seen.

'Jesus, Grant, fuck - did you need to do that! This mission is wrong; it's so fucked up. If we're stooping to killing unarmed men now what's wrong with putting two shots in his chest?'

Grant sneered as he turned to look James in the eye.

'You damn well knew what you signed up for — and who the fuck do you think you are anyway!' Grant snapped back, jabbing the end of his rifle twice into James' chest.

'How's that for two in the fucking chest!'

'Whoa, whoa, easy Lt, let it go,' said Mark, carefully placing his hand on the end of Grant's rifle and lowering it. The muzzle was hot and sticky with the man's blood, and Mark felt embarrassed when he touched it.

'I'll tell you when I'll let it go. I'm fucking in charge; do you all understand?' Grant yelled, glancing around the group.

'If any of you want to take over, go for it. Right now, right fucking here. But I warn you - even if you beat me, I'll be the best runner up you've ever had!'

He took a deep breath, then looked at each soldier in turn. Rocky and Mark immediately looked away, but James held his gaze a little too long, and Grant strode forward, quickly closing the gap between them. Grant was certainly not going to stand for this. It was his mission, even if that meant killing unarmed men to get it done; they would do as they were fucking well told or they'd soon regret it. His breath washed over James' face like a wave of hate making him think better of saying anything else. Grant's face contorted with rage, flecks of spittle forming in the corners his mouth as he breathed through clenched teeth. James stared down at the ground tilting his head, refusing to meet Grant's eye, like a dog afraid of his master's boot.

'Didn't think so,' Grant said, with a hint of mockery in his voice, before turning to look at the other soldiers.

'You two, got a fucking problem following orders?' Rocky checked that his grenades were securely attached to his combat vest then shook his head, shifting his weight from one leg to another before turning away to scan the area through his scope.

'All good here,' answered Mark, wiping his hand on his trousers as he looked down at the ruined face of the man Grant had killed.

Satisfied that his chain of command was well and truly restored, Grant's anger subsided almost as rapidly as it had appeared.

'Okay,' he said, 'this mission is obviously compromised now. The gas should have taken care of these fuckers, but not all the rockets have activated properly.'

Grant began rambling, sounding as if he was speaking his thoughts aloud as he wandered around, his boots leaving a trail of overlapping small circles in the dusty ground.

'Weapons inspectors will crawl all over here soon… that's good… good... that's okay… that's the whole point of the mission… but… witnesses… we can't leave behind any witnesses… shit… shit... okay.'

Finally, he stopped pacing and looked up at his team. His decision was made.

'Right asshole you're coming with me,' he said shoving James towards the house where the first set of rockets had landed, 'and any more of that shit and I'll put two in your fucking chest.'

'You two, clear that house over there,' he told Rocky and Mike, pointing his rifle to the boys' house, 'find the kids, put them down then meet us back at the RV for exfil.'

James took point — the bullet catchers position, with Grant following a short distance behind him. James was more worried about a bullet from behind than any that might come from elsewhere as they had already taken care of the only man they'd seen from their observation post.

The sun was threatening to rise, its dull pre-dawn red glow turning the snow-topped mountains into a mess of blood and shattered bones. He was reasonably sure that there would be no mines buried near to the houses, but James still patrolled cautiously, his boots making soft crunching noises in the dry sandy ground.

He didn't see her at first in the dim light. From a distance, he thought it was another cluster of rocks, but as he drew closer, the shape revealed itself to be a woman, curled up in the foetal position, her fists clenched tight and claw-like against her stomach.

'Lt, over here,' James called out. Grant startled him when he appeared next to him almost straight away. They stood at the side of her, looking down, awaiting Grants judgement.

'Well, would you look at this ugly bitch — shoot her.'

'She's gone, why don't we leave her,' James said, then froze when he felt the muzzle of Grant's rifle press against the base of his skull.

'I've warned you. What did I tell you about messing me around? Shoot the bitch - that's a damned order!'

Before James could protest further, they heard a faint whimper, then a sad moan coming from somewhere over to their right.

'Funny, the gas should have taken care of everybody over this end,' Grant said, pushing James out of the way to shoot the woman, her body jerking twice as the bullets slammed into her chest.

'You really are a fucking pussy,' Grant said, fixing James with a disappointing stare before stalking off toward the source of the noise.

At first, Amira didn't recognise the noise she heard, the effects of the gas and being laid on the cold ground for such a long time had messed up her sense of reality.

Amira was too weak to move, she thought she could hear Hana's voice carried by the breeze, whispering riddles to her. Amira could hear her right now, Hana was walking over to her, she listened to the footsteps grow louder as she got nearer. She had last seen Hana crawling around like a dying animal; perhaps she had got better and was coming over to help.

Amira was confused. She was sure that Hana was dead.

She couldn't be alive, could she? Had she left her friend too soon? Amira's confusion gave way to fear when she realised that the noise was coming from not one, but two people walking towards her. They were approaching her, trying to be quiet, but their footsteps made gentle crunching sounds as they walked on the coarse sandy ground.

One of them kicked a small rock, and she heard them curse; it was a man's voice. It wasn't Hana, it couldn't be now, and they were getting closer and closer to her. She lay as still as she could, but the cold or the gas made her shiver uncontrollably.

Perhaps they hadn't seen her. Not daring to turn her head in case the motion drew attention to her, Amira looked out of the corner of her eyes and saw the shapes of two men approaching. The vomit on her face had dried; she could still smell it, and her stomach acid or something else had burned her throat, making it painful to breathe. As well as the sharp odour of bile, there was another smell, and when Amira remembered that she had wet and soiled herself, she felt ashamed.

As she lay on the cold ground, taking shallow wheezy breaths, she felt something pressing on her chest, a slight weight, nothing too heavy. It felt like the weight of an infant, she reasoned with herself, and when she felt the faint warm breath of the boy on her neck, an intense terror gripped her.

The first soldier was so near now; it would only be moments before he saw her. She dared not move, but she knew she had to keep the child safe. Amira reached out with her right hand, it was numb, and she swept it over the ground, struggling to find a rock to hurl at them to keep the child safe. She could hear their hushed, urgent voices now. They were so close. Her fingers skimmed over a rock, and she grasped at it, but her hand wouldn't close around it, and it slipped from her weak grip. She knew then she would die tonight, but instead of self-pity, Amira was filled with a rage she had never felt before, and she desperately reached out for the rock again, but her outstretched fingers couldn't find it. Protecting the child was the only thing that mattered to Amira now, the only thing she could think about. As she tried to move her hand back to shelter the boy, something stopped her from doing so. Her hand had become snagged in the cords of one of the rocket's parachutes which had strayed off course. Amira laboriously untangled her hand, and with the last ounces of strength in her body, she leaned towards the parachute and shoved the unconscious child underneath its canvas.

Grant reached her first.
'Well, would you look at this pretty little one. I'd give her a hoodsie. Well, you know if she wasn't dead and covered in shit.' Grant smirked, lifting her skirts up with

the end of his rifle. Grant looked at James mistaking his disgusted expression for confusion.

'Hoodsie, it's a Boston thing, I'm sure you've tried one with that nice wife of yours. No? Well try one sometime - I think you'd both like it,' he said with an odd grin.

James shrugged his shoulders, unsure of what Grant was talking about, and they stared awkwardly at each other before a burst of gunfire from the other house shattered the silence. They recognised it at once, the distinctive rattle of an AK47 assault rifle.

'Jesus, fuck! What now? Why do I have to work with you useless assholes,' Grant yelled, raising his rifle to look through the scope at the direction of the noise.

James glanced down at the woman on the ground and is shocked to see her looking right at him, her eyes wide and unblinking. Without moving her head, the woman's eyes drift to the right, and James follows her gaze. He sees then what she's looking at; a child partially covered by the parachute. Checking that Grant is still looking the other way, James put his boot under the fabric and drags it until the canvas completely covers the child. When James looks back down at the woman, she is smiling at him; her mouth is moving, thanking him, although he can't understand her softly spoken words.

Grant lowered his sight and looked down at Amira, 'shame,' he says, before shooting her twice in the chest then turning and running in the direction of the other house.

CHAPTER TWELVE

9

Before this, before everything, I read somewhere that you can hear people talking to you when you are in a coma. Well, just so you know it's true. Well, sort of. I listen to them sometimes. Their words come and go. I don't think anybody talks 'to' me, but I hear them talking about me. Other times they talk about what they want to eat or where they want to go. Sometimes I know they are talking, but I can't make out what they are saying. Maybe they are speaking in a code or a different language on purpose. I hear something now. I can hear footsteps coming towards me.

CHAPTER THIRTEEN

Holdfast

'Goran, what was that noise? Come see at the window,' said Salim as he peered out of the window into the valley.

'What is it?'

Salim pulled him down roughly by his shoulder, 'I don't know, I thought I heard shouting — look, men are coming — soldiers I think, Goran go get father from his room, be quick!'

Salim watched the soldiers approaching, advancing rapidly towards the house. Goran returned with the Kalashnikov, 'father is not there. Where has he gone Salim!'

'I don't know,' Salim replied, dragging him into the corner of the room to hide by their beds. There was no time to give the rifle to Salim who was the better shot. Goran pulled the weapon into his shoulder, trying to remember how to hold it properly, his rapid breathing causing the muzzle to rise and fall by six inches each time he took a breath. Goran closed his eyes for a moment and managed to calm himself, trying to block out the fear. He looked around the room and tried to hold his breath to steady the rifle, but when he did his nervous shaking made it worse. The heavy gun slipped in his palms and beads of sweat stung his eyes, but he dared not take his hand off the rifle to wipe it away in case he had to shoot. The boys shivered as they waited in silence crouched together behind their beds.

It was only a slight sound, but it was enough to break the silence. They heard a dull creaking noise as the door to their house was slowly opened and they knew instantly that the soldiers were searching for them downstairs.

'Goran let's climb down, out of the window,' Salim whispered.

'It's too high if we fall, we'll get hurt — and what if there are more of them outside?'

'Nonsense, come, we have done it many times. Stand up and move. Now!' He urged.

Goran stood up slowly, seemingly unsure of what to do. Salim turned back from the window and grabbed his brother by the shoulder, pulling him to towards the window but as he moved, the heavy rifle slipped from his grasp and clattered loudly on the stone floor. Fear paralysed him, and he froze in a half-standing half-crouching position unsure what to do. He looked at Salim and watched him hold a finger to his lips for him to be quiet. They remained still, listening, waiting and expecting the soldiers to burst into the room any second. But they didn't. The soldiers didn't come. Puzzled, Goran looked at his brother and shrugged his shoulders. Perhaps they thought better of it now they knew they that the boys had a gun and could defend themselves. But then they heard it. It was almost undetectable - the soft sound of footsteps moving up the stairs, the scrape of equipment against the wall. The soldiers were professional, moving slowly and methodically, trying not to make a noise, but the children had played this game hundreds of times in the past and recognised the sounds. They knew the soldiers would be there soon.

The world was a green haze for the soldiers as they looked through their passive night-vision goggles. The house would have been pitch black without them, but with the aid of the embers of the near-dead fire, they could see clearly enough to make their way around the furniture and not disturb the toys and clutter on the stairs as they neared the source of the noise. Their pre-deployment intelligence briefings had prepared them thoroughly, and they had a good understanding of how the houses in this area were laid out. The soldiers arrived at the top of the stairs after only making cursory checks of the downstairs rooms; there was no need to; they could recognise the sound of a weapon being dropped. All soldiers could. If you were unlucky enough for it to be you doing the dropping, you would be severely disciplined— both financially and physically enough that it was unlikely that you dropped one again.

The boys knew where the soldiers were — they were right outside the room now.

Salim tiptoed quickly across the room, picked up the gun and held it with the stock under his arm to steady it as he waited for them, all the hours spent learning to shoot accurately now totally forgotten.

Rocky found himself at the top of the stairs first and pointed to one of Mark's stun grenades and then to the door. They had practised room clearances and fighting in built-up areas many times. It was usually hard and physically demanding work. But this was their first time against children. Should be a piece of cake. Mark took hold of the grenade and held on to the fly-off lever, dropping the pin to the floor. It bounced once on the bare stone floor making hardly any noise at all. But it was enough for the boys to hear. Salim burst from the room down the corridor and pulled the trigger of the AK47 until no more bullets came. The rifle was out of control and bullets struck the nearest soldier, first in the ankle, then the top of the thigh and twice in the neck as the recoil made the rifle rise. As soon as the bullets hit his neck, they severed the carotid artery; blood sprayed from the wound in spectacular pulses leaving fan-like patterns on the wall. The soldiers face hit the wall, and he slumped forward ending up as a crumpled mess on the floor.

People think when you get shot you end up on your back or front, but spend any time in a war zone, and you know this couldn't be further from the truth — the dead end up in all sorts of positions; limbs twisted and bent, face down with their ass in the air like a sleeping baby and every conceivable combination between.

The blood loss was rapid, and he was dead before his body came to rest on the floor, so fast that there was no time for his life to flash before him. Rocky never imagined that his life would end in a dirty Kurdish house in the middle of nowhere, then again neither did his mother or steroid supplier for that matter.

Caught by surprise, Mark dropped the stun grenade and flung himself out of the way of the hail of 7.62 mm bullets from the AK47 and clambered into the corner of the bedroom with barely enough time to clamp his eyes shut.

Salim looked at the cylindrical thing that the soldier had dropped, then a split second later he shouted out in pain as the stun grenade went off. The flash of light was brighter than anything he had ever seen. Every sensory pigment in his retina suddenly activated making vision impossible. It was like being blinded by the sun but being unable to look away to avoid its intense light. The 'bang' was worse though. Salim dropped the AK47 and held his hands to his ears stumbling around like a drunk, unsteady on his feet as the blast disturbed the balance in the pressure of the fluid in his ear canals. He felt like he had been punched in the face and cried out for his brother who grabbed him, throwing his arms around him hugging him tightly.

'It's alright my brother, it's okay,' Salim said to Goran although they could not see or hear each other.

But Goran was not okay; he was shaking and ashamed as a hot trickle of urine ran down his legs to pool at his feet as fear made him wet himself.

CHAPTER FOURTEEN
Broken Limbs

Mark had dived into the room as soon as he heard the first blast of gunfire and found himself on the floor wedged awkwardly up against the heavy wooden end of a bed. Shuffling around to sit upright, he took his weight on both hands but cried out in agony as his right arm collapsed under him. The tapestry of faceless men looked down on him unsympathetically. He felt cold and sick as shock took hold of him and he threw up when he raised his arm and saw it hanging limply in his sleeve. His right arm had been cut in half by a bullet that had ricocheted from the wall as he took cover. Confused, he stared at his arm and the odd shapes that the shattered bones formed — some were held in by the clothing, but others stuck out through the ripped fabric like broken shards of dirty white glass. Mark fumbled with the chinstrap of his helmet, unclipping it and letting it drop to the floor before drawing his rifle close to him, convincing himself that the mission is still viable. Get out of the house alive then get out of this God-damned country. Not realising that he had retrieved it, he felt the reassuring weight of his rifle resting on his thighs. He looked to see if the magazine was still attached. It is. Then Mark ran his hand further down the barrel to check that silencer is still screwed on. Not that it matters about being silent anymore, the time for that has passed. The metal of the slim barrel feels cool to the touch but before he reaches the silencer his fingers find a slight dent and crack in the barrel where a bullet has glanced off it. There was no hole there, but he knows if he shoots his rifle now, there might not be enough gas pressure to force the bullet out, or worse still, it could jam in there causing the pressure to build up too high, making the bullet explode in the barrel which would kill him. Listening to the sounds and movement just outside the door, he lurches to his feet pulling out his combat knife from its sheath before walking unsteadily out of the room.

Still holding his brother tight, through blurred eyes over his brother's shoulder Salim sees the soldier emerge from the bedroom and he forces his brother along the landing towards the stairs.

'Go! Run!' He yells, shoving Goran down the stairs. 'Goran, find father.' Salim shouts again to his brother who is already halfway down.

The soldier rushes towards Salim but as he steps over the lifeless bulk of his teammate, he slips in a pool of blood and stumbles, sending the knife flying past Salim. Salim moves quickly to pick up the knife, it is heavier than he expected and in his small hands it looks enormous. The blade is made of non-reflective black metal which curves to a sharp point and on the back jagged teeth run down it like a saw.

Salim is suddenly knocked off his feet as the soldier violently slams into him, and the soldier who must be at least 150 pounds heavier, lands on top pinning the child to the floor. There is a muffled crack as Salim's ribs break and he screams out in agony. He gasps for air as he struggles to breathe, feeling the equipment attached to the soldier's tactical vest pressing hard into his ribcage. The soldier grabs hold of Salim's windpipe with one hand, crushing and twisting and pulling frantically. Within moments, Salim sees stars as he is starved of oxygen. The soldier's breath is hot and wet on his face and he can feel the soldier's heartbeat through his equipment. The soldier's eyes are wide with fury as he looks straight into Salim's eyes. They say the eyes are a window to the soul, but what Salim saw in that man's eyes was no soul he wanted to see.

On the verge of passing out, Salim hears a noise, but it takes him a moment to figure out where it is coming from. It's the scraping sound that the tip of the knife is making as he drags it over the stone floor towards the soldier. Darkness swirls around his consciousness, but before it claims him, Salim jabs the knife into the soldier's leg, pushing hard until it hits a bone. The soldier gasps in shock and pain, sending spittle onto the boy's face as he shifts away from the sharp stinging pain of the knife. Shards of bone from his ruined arm tear into his skin as he tries to escape the blade. Air floods back into Salim's lungs, and he pulls the knife out in a twisting motion and then continues stabbing the man's legs, hips, stomach — anywhere he can. A jarring pain shoots up Salim's arm from the impact of striking the man's pelvis. Blood slithers under his fingers making his grip slip, but he keeps stabbing the soldier until he has no power left in his arm. The knife drops to the floor and a calm sensation comes over Salim as he lays still, not feeling or hearing the soldier's heartbeat anymore. The only thing he felt at that moment was hot blood oozing out of the dead soldier and soaking into his clothes, which, for some reason was surprisingly comforting.

Sweat stung Salim's eyes as he pushed pathetically at the dead weight of the soldier still half sprawled across him; clawing at the soldiers clothing trying to shift him until he has no strength left. Salim lets out a loud laugh as he struggles in vain to adjust his position underneath the dead man. The blood cools rapidly on the cold stone floor, and Salim is amazed at the amount he can see. The coppery flavour of blood lingers in his mouth, and he wonders if it is all his as he runs his tongue over a split lip.

The sombre light of dawn begins to creep in through the upstairs windows; its fingers illuminating the macabre paintings on the pale white walls. The blood looks almost black on the walls as it seems to absorb the growing daylight and Salim notices some blood has made it onto the ceiling. It is as silent as a tomb until the quiet is broken by a fly buzzing around his face before settling on the soldiers back and turning to consider Salim, rubbing its legs together in glad anticipation of something.

The darkness of sleep tugs at him - he is exhausted. Salim fights against it, struggling to keep his eyes open as he absently draws small circles in the congealing blood with his fingers. The fly lands on his broken lip, pausing there before crawling over his cheek towards his eye.

How long will it take for father to come? He must have heard all this noise.

There is a creaking noise as the door to the house slowly opens, Salim's eyes snap open, and he lets out a pathetic laugh.

'Up here Papa, help me!' he yells and waits for his father to shout back and rush up the stairs.

But he hears no rushing, no urgent shouts from his father.

Confused, Salim shouts again, 'I'm up here!'

Nothing.

Then.

'Oh, I know where you are little boy,' replies the American as he walks up the stairs.

'You fucking people,' he says as he walks.

'…Saddam should have gassed the lot of you…'

The voice grows louder.

'…in the eighties…'

Louder still.

'… done the whole damn world a favour… '

At the top of the stairs now.

'… wouldn't have had to come to this shit hole.'

Salim sees him now at the top of the stairs standing by the crumpled mess that was once a member of his team; once a person, perhaps somebody's father. The soldier reaches for the man's neck which Salim finds strange, surely he knows he's dead, no need to check for a pulse. With a jerk, the soldier pulls out the dead man's dog-tags, wipes them on his trousers and puts them into his pocket.

It's surprising how much blood the human body contains — what is more surprising is how much more it looks like once outside of the body. Grant nods at the amount of it. He had seen plenty of men (and women) bleed out before and caused a fair share blood loss over the years, but this was something else. He was impressed. The arterial spray of blood over the walls looked like somebody had thrown entire paint tins of the stuff around. In the early grey light of dawn, the dark colour of blood was a stark contrast to the pale bone colour of the wall. Grant thought it looked beautiful. He stepped over his fallen comrade smiling to himself, enjoying the feeling as his boots squelched in the sticky congealing blood on the floor.

'Well, well,' he says, as he kneels next to the boy.

'Who'd a thought a little skinny asshole like you could have done all of this,' he continues, taking in the human carnage in front of him: the blood, shattered bones, the dead members of his team.

'This one will take a little creative explanation when I get back to base won't it?' He says to the boy as he leans closer to his face, studying his features.

'Ahh, don't cry, it'll be over soon,' Grant says, reaching out with his left hand to wipe the boy's tears away.

Salim seizes his chance, and he strikes out to slash the man's face. The soldier sees the knife at the last possible moment and staggers backwards to avoid the sharp blade. With his right hand still gripping his rifle, Grant has no choice but to thrust out his left hand for balance, and the blade hits the middle of his little finger, practically severing it. Salim strikes out again, but the knife slips from his hand and he frantically grabs for it, but the soldier lets out an odd laugh as he kicks the heavy blade away from his desperate fingers.

The soldier stood over the boy, looking at his finger, the end of it hanging at an obscene angle, still attached by a thin sliver of skin.

'You little motherfucker!' Grant shouts as he looks down at the boy. All those firefights he'd been in over the years Grant had never gotten so much as a scratch. And now this little fuck had cut half of his finger off with one of his men's own knives.

Salim's eyes are wide open, not with fear Grant

71

realises, but with defiance and he has to fight the urge to kill the boy right then. Grant opens his mouth to speak but stops when he hears the metallic clatter of the high-explosive grenade Salim had taken from the soldier's vest, slip from his grip to the floor. Grant doesn't seem concerned; he shakes his head as he scoops up the hand grenade and holds it up in front of Salim.

'No so cocky now are you boy? Do you know these things have a four-second delay before they explode?' He says, tapping the grenade against the boy's head.

'But you're supposed to pull the pin out — you stupid cunt,' he says, shaking the grenade, making the circular ring of the pin rattle against the smooth green body of the grenade.

'Are you ready?' Grant says before pulling out the pin and releasing the fly-off lever.

'Here we go.'

'One.'

Salim shouts, pleading for his life.

'Two.'

The shouts from the boy stop, and he stares at the soldier, eyes wide with fear now, all defiance gone.

'Three.'

Salim squeezes his eyes so tight he sees stars as he

waits to die. Grant smirks as he throws the hand grenade down the stairs into the main living area. It bounces off the last stair and skids over the floor ending up almost in the dead centre of the room. The hand grenade explodes a fraction of a second later with a loud crack, releasing its deadly metal fragments in a 360-degree radius; throwing its pressure wave out into the room and up the stairs. Salim's hair is blown back from his forehead, and he feels grit and heat wash over him like a blast of hot air.

'Didn't think I'd let it go off up here, did you? Who knows, maybe that's taken care of one of you lot hiding downstairs.'

Grant watches the boy's eyes flitting everywhere, desperately searching for someone to help him, to help him escape, but there is no one coming to save him.

Salim prays quietly, 'Bavê me yê li ezmanan, Bila navê te p" roz be,' he repeatedly mutters, looking straight into the soldier's eyes. He sees the soldier frown, and then Salim watches him stand — picking up the AK47 as he does so, before he takes off its curved magazine and slowly pulls back the cocking handle.

'Ah the last bullet is jammed in, look see,' he says, turning the rifle over showing Salim the inside of the magazine housing before ejecting the jammed bullet and catching it mid-air.

'Do you know the AK47 was designed to be very reliable, to work even if dirty and poorly maintained...' Grant's nose screws up in disappointment at the condition of the weapon, '... like this one is? Betcha did, and they are you know, it's my opinion that this particular weapon — your AK47, this one here, would work for years. Think of all the goats, or whatever shit you people shoot at, you could kill.'

'Problem is,' he continues as he slots the bullet back into the magazine and clips it back onto the weapon, 'is the cheap ammunition that doesn't load properly. Poor old Mikhail would turn in his grave if he knew how his beloved creation was being disrespected.'

Grant pulled back and released the cocking handle which made a surprisingly loud noise in the confined space of the landing.

'There we go, all loaded and ready to fire,' he said in a slightly theatrical voice. He looks at Salim.

'Are you ready?' he says flatly.

The boy had stopped praying; there was no point anymore. His God had either not heard his prayers; or if he had, he had chosen to ignore them — and it was too late now anyway. What Grant would remember for the rest of his life was the disgust he saw in that boy's eyes, and of course, the fear and resignation in the split second before he crushed his throat with the chipped wooden stock of his father's AK47.

CHAPTER FIFTEEN

Blue on Blue

Goran fled down the stairs to get away from the soldier with the big knife. He ran so fast that he slammed into the door at the bottom of the stairs which led out into the yard. He had avoided the full brunt of the stun grenade, but his ears still hurt a little from the noise, and he had been a little blinded by the bright light which had penetrated the room. It was as if he had looked at the sun for too long and he saw a bright blur wherever he looked.

Goran slammed the door shut and rested his back against the rough wooden surface while he thought about what to do next, where to go. He was surprised that his father hadn't come back yet — perhaps he'd been cut off by the soldiers and had stayed at Hana's house to protect the women as they knew Salim would keep him safe. Well, he was safe now, but Salim wasn't; he was still in there with him. Goran knew that he shouldn't have left him to fight the soldier alone, but Salim had practically thrown him down the stairs to get him out of danger. Goran turned and took hold of the door handle to go back into the house to help, but as much as he tried, he could not bring himself to open the door. His pyjama trousers stuck to the wetness between his legs giving him a physical reminder of his fear. His father would know what to do he thought, as he set out to find him, blinking rapidly trying to bring his normal vision back as he ran away from the house.

Goran had only gone a short distance when he saw a long cylindrical metal object in front of him, and he stopped dead in his tracks, surprised to see it there. It wasn't there last night before he went to sleep, and he hadn't heard it land. He reached out warily to touch the cold metal surface, and as he looked around, the pale light of the breaking dawn revealed more of the same objects scattered about on the ground. He saw that most were intact, but the one near to the animal enclosure seemed to have broken in half, and all the animals in there lay lifeless on the ground. Puzzled, Goran stood up to move away, and as he did so, he saw people coming to help him. One, no two people are running towards him from the direction of Hana's house.

'Papa,' he wants to call out to them, but when he recognises the silhouettes as the shapes of soldiers, he manages to stop himself just in time.

Unable to run away in case he is seen, Goran does the only thing that he can think of, he lays down, stretching out as long as possible, his body close to the object to avoid being seen. He dared not look. Goran clasps his hands tight over his eyes as if not being able to see the soldiers will make him invisible to them.

If you looked out from the house, he would be seen with his off-white pyjamas, and brown hair highlighted clearly against the colour of the rocket, but the soldiers aren't looking for anybody there, and they run past without seeing him. When he eventually forces himself to peek out through small gaps in his fingers, he sees one soldier quietly open the door and enter his house while the other moves around the back out of sight.

Goran lay still for what seemed an age before he dared get up to continue to Hana's house. He watched cautiously as he slowly stood up, keeping his eyes on his home in case the soldier who hadn't gone in came back and saw him. Finally, just as Goran summoned the courage to move, he saw the door to his house fly off violently as something exploded loudly inside. The only thing left of the door was its thick metal hinges, which hung limp and bent in the door frame. Dust belched out through the open space and from the upstairs windows, and within seconds the soldier from behind the house returned and was shouting at somebody inside the house. Goran heard an angry reply shouted back, then the soldier nodded and turned to look right at him, and seconds later Goran fell as he was shot.

Grant had seen the boy stand up and he swore, annoyed that he had missed him; how could the little shit have evaded them, they were a SEAL team for God's sake, the best of the fucking best.

'You people are severely testing my patience,' he said to himself, grinding his teeth together as he felt the rage building up inside of him.

He raised his rifle and took aim, his mouth forming a thin smile when he saw the boys scared face looking up at him, enlarged in the centre of his crosshairs. Lowering his aim slightly he squeezed the trigger gently and saw blood spray from the boy's chest as the force of the bullet flung him backwards over the rocket like a ragdoll. Grant heard James shout something from below and then watched with amusement as he saw him sprint over to the boy, pulling out his first aid kit as he went.

'Ah, well isn't that nice, the pussy wants to keep your brother alive. Well - I assume he's your brother but who knows with you inbred fuckers.' Grant said to the dead boy on the floor, who stared back with unblinking bloodshot eyes — there was no defiance in them now. Grant rested his hand on the window ledge as he looked out to see James kneeling over the boy, his first aid kit wide open as he frantically searched for morphine and a field dressing to treat the boy.

'No need to waste the good old US of A taxpayer's money by wasting that medical kit on him now is there soldier,' Grant whispers as he aims at James, sighting his crosshairs in the centre of his back.

Grant takes up the first trigger pressure and slows his breathing to focus on making sure that the shot will hit him in the dead centre of his back; he was a marksman after all, and he took pride in his killing. Grant was about to pull the trigger then he stopped abruptly.

'Can't do it.' he said aloud.

'This is wrong.'

'No, can't do it with my weapon — that would just be wrong wouldn't it,' he says as he carefully leans his rifle against the wall and picks up the AK47.

'Don't you go messing with my rifle now dead boy,' he warns as he looks over the iron sights of the AK47 at his target.

'Alright then, one shot, one kill,' he says, as he pulls the trigger to shoot James in the back.

CHAPTER SIXTEEN
Provide Comfort

The Royal Marines have always fought with distinction right from their formation in 1664 when they were first known as the Duke of York and Albany's Maritime Regiment of Foot. They have battle honours stretching back centuries, and their levels of fitness are legendary, as they superbly demonstrated during the Falklands War. Following the sinking of the Atlantic Conveyor, and with it all of their troop-carrying helicopters, the Marines then had to carry their 100-pound Bergan's over great distances before engaging the enemy. In a time when politicians were looking to disband the Royal Marines or perhaps merge them with Army's Parachute Regiment, the retaking of the Falkland Islands put to bed any question of this, thus securing the future of the elite 8000 strong marine corps.

As a fast-moving amphibious force, the Royal Marines had few armoured combat vehicles, and it was for this reason they had not been called upon nine years later to become part of the land offensive in the Gulf War.

Intelligence suggested that the war would be fought in the desert with military planners favouring fast-moving armoured units. The Royal Marines biggest strength, their ability to conduct raids launched from the sea and then march to their target, was thought to be of little use in an armoured assault in the vast desert. Desperate to have some involvement, commanders had reluctantly accepted to deploy, not as an attacking force, but in a humanitarian role in anticipation of the need to deal with the swarms of civilians who would flee to the relative safety of Syria and Northern Iraq until the war was over.

'Operation Haven' was the public name for the joint British and American effort to support the resettlement of the population uprooted by war. It was intended to be a classic 'hearts and minds' approach that had been successfully used by the British all over the world in far-flung places such as Borneo, and, depending on the accent of the person you were talking with, to some extent in Northern Ireland. The American approach to winning 'hearts and minds' conjures up images of napalm drops and children fleeing from burning villages so it was decided that they would be responsible for providing logistic support only.

Reconnaissance teams made up of Royal Marines, and civilian aid workers had been established to carry out air-to-ground inspections of potential field hospitals and refugee processing centres in Southern Turkey and Northern Iraq. In command of one such team was Royal Marine Colour Sergeant Ivan Hawley, a veteran of 19 years' service. He had been involved in three tours of Northern Ireland during the controversial 'shoot to kill' era and had seen fierce fighting in the Falkland's War for which he was awarded the Military Medal. Ivan had been part of a fighting patrol that found itself in an Argentinian minefield before becoming pinned down by an enemy machine gun position. Ivan crawled through the minefield to the Argentineans position, taking it out by throwing white phosphorous grenades into the bunker and then jumping into the trench to shoot the enemy soldiers. Once the battle for Mount Harriet was over and the minefield was made safe, it turned out that Ivan had crawled almost five hundred metres to the bunker and over two mines which had not detonated. Despite approaching forty years of age, he was still a formidable character; despite being only five foot eight and slightly built he commanded the respect of marines and officers alike. He was looking forward to retiring in three years and hoped that this would be his last deployment.

Satisfied that they had achieved their objective for the day, Ivan spoke into the microphone of his headset and told the American pilot of the Black Hawk helicopter to turn around and head back to their base in Southern Turkey. He looked around at his team made up of three marines and two volunteer medics from 'Doctors without Borders', who they had to protect while they carried out their ground surveys. His marines looked irritated; baby-sitting civilians was not what they had completed eight months of arduous basic training for, while Dominic Fuller and Jim Dunn, the two aid workers attached to his team, looked utterly exhausted. The early starts, late finishes and the constant bone-rattling vibrations of the helicopter's rotors could wear you out if you were not used to it. Hell, they wore you down even if you were used to it. There had been teething problems as you might expect when making elite fighting troops work with civilians who had different ideas and approaches, but Ivan had been impressed with Dominic and Jim. They had always turned up early, well prepared for the day's tasks and conducted themselves in a professional manner; they were a real credit to the Manchester Royal Infirmary, the hospital which had let them have time off to take part in the operation. As experienced Accident and Emergency Doctors, Dominic and Jim's experience might be useful should they be called upon to treat any refugees who might need it.

Bodies strained against shoulder straps as the helicopter banked sharply to the right as it changed direction and increased its speed at the same time to head away from their base in Turkey. The aid workers held on tight and anxiously watched Ivan's face for clues of what might be happening as he listened to the message from the pilot. They watched him look at his marines as he said something into the headset before he removed it and hesitated briefly before shouting over the din of the rotors.

'We've been re-tasked - American SF team are in trouble, get ready, could be a hot LZ,' he shouted to his marines who were already busy checking their equipment and ammunition.

'We'll need you two as well — sounds like they have casualties,' he shouted to the medics.

CHAPTER SEVENTEEN

8

People cry, not because they're weak. It's because they've been strong for far too long.

CHAPTER EIGHTEEN
Optical Illusions

Grant sat on top of the rocket and looked down at James lying face down on the ground next to the boy. He had shot James almost dead centre in his back; the bullet had split his sternum, the force of it stopping his heart instantly. Grant then examined the boy's face, he looked younger close-up but then again being dead strips away the years he thought to himself. The boy didn't have a pained expression, if anything, he looked peaceful; his eyes were closed, and his mouth had formed an "O" shape, which Grant found amusing. Better call it in he thought as he looked down at James' sprawled body; his arms stretched over his head like he was surrendering. He still had hold of an open field dressing, its white bandages a useless flag of surrender as they lay on the dusty ground.

'Zero, Zero, this is November Three Four, contact wait out,' Grant yelled into his radio.

He waited for a moment before sending an update; he could just imagine them all staring at maps and huddled around the radio waiting for more information from him. The smell of sweat and tension in the crowded operations tent would be palpable. Grant pressed the send button of his radio intermittently as he shouted orders and let off a few rounds of ammunition. The broken messages combined with the weapon noises would be getting them nicely worked up now.

'Zero, Zero, request immediate exfil at my location over,' Grant said into the radio in a muffled tone to make them think he was hiding behind cover.

'Negative November Three Four, proceed to original exfil coordinates, over.'

Grant didn't reply.

'November Three Four, confirm my last, over.'

'Negative, negative, need exfil at my location — we have multiple casualties, repeat multiple casualties, over. Grant replied.

'November Three Four, say again, say again, over.'

'Zero, we have multiple fucking casualties, multiple casualties, get us out of here now!' Grant shouted as he released a burst of automatic fire into the air.

'November Three Four, roger, wait out.'

Grant walked over to James, peeling his fingers back

to prise the field dressing from his hand and drop it onto his back.

'Waste not want not I say James.' Grant said as he looked around taking in the view of the mountains, the thin coating of snow gleaming brightly in the morning sunlight. It was shaping up to be a really lovely day.

'November Three Four, November Three Four, send sitrep, over.'

Grant paused, he would have to get his story straight; say the right things and he would become a hero, medals and promotions would surely follow. Say the wrong thing, and he would look incompetent, the officer who got his entire team killed — not that they had needed much help in that matter. Experienced soldiers, SEAL's taken out by children for fuck's sake. No, there would be plenty of time to come up with something convincing before the official debrief, after all he'd gotten away with it before in Panama. He looked down at his damaged finger, somewhere in all the excitement the tip had detached.

'Zero, Zero, this is November Three Four, our team was engaged as we investigated defective package, the enemy has bugged out, but we have three casualties... repeat three casualties, over.'

'November Three Four, roger. Standby for extraction by friendly forces. British team at your location in figures two five, two five over.'

'Zero, roger, out,' Grant said, grinning as he twirled James' dog-tags around his index finger before resting them on James' back so that he could rub sand into his eyes.

The helicopter pilot had pushed his machine to the limits, and they arrived ten minutes later, circling once before landing, throwing up a cloud of dirt and scattering small stones in a wide circle. Ivan slid open the side door of the helicopter and was out before the helicopter's wheels had touched the ground, quickly followed by his marines. The marines hastily took up defensive positions at the front and rear of the helicopter as Ivan and the medics ran towards a soldier who seemed to be treating someone. As they grew closer, they saw some kind of rocket and Grant pressing a filthy bandage onto James' back next to a dead child.

'What happened?' Ivan said, taking in the surrounding scene, searching for potential enemy positions. Grant didn't reply.

'Hey, come away let the medics see,' Ivan said, tugging on Grant's shoulder to move him out of the way.

Grant slapped Ivan's arm aside, 'the boys gone, I couldn't save him,' Grant said, looking up at Ivan, his eyes were damp and red as if he had been crying and there was blood on his cheeks where he had wiped the tears away.

'We were just an observation post up there,' Grant nodded towards the mountains, 'when we saw these things float down, so we came down to see what they were,' Grant lied.

'Then we got ambushed and the kids, the kids, they… they got caught up in the crossfire,' he continued, his voice breaking.

'Did you see anybody on your flight in, they broke contact with me about 10 minutes before you showed up. Probably ran out of ammo or went for reinforcements.'

Ivan shook his head as he took in the scene around him. Missiles or rockets, dead soldiers and children, this was supposed to be a quiet tour. If the media got hold of this, it would cause a shit storm back in the UK.

A voice from behind, Dominic the medic said in a thick northern accent, 'he's been shot in the spine — he won't be walking again, poor sod'll probably never even bloody wake up.'

'Come on, let's get you out of here,' Ivan said to Grant. The medics had loaded James onto a portable stretcher and awkwardly walked towards the helicopter struggling with the dead weight of a soldier and his combat equipment.

'No, I can't, I've got men in the house. No one gets left behind,' Grant said, staring blankly at Ivan.

'It's all right, there's already follow up teams in the air on the way - your guys, Americans, they'll be here soon to get your team out I promise,' Ivan said as he squeezed Grants shoulder, 'but look we need to leave, to get him help,' Ivan said looking at medics loading the soldier into the helicopter.

'Okay,' Grant mumbled.

'Okay, can we go?'

Grant nodded and then they ran towards the helicopter, ducking down as they approached the rotor blades. The medics had already got a drip into James' arm and were kneeling over him busily checking for other injuries. Ivan got in first and held out his hand to help Grant who ignored the gesture. Moments later his marines were on board, and the helicopter was taking off.

'Don't worry, we'll save him,' Ivan shouted towards Grant.

'I fucking hope not,' Grant whispered, confident he wouldn't be heard over the roar of the rotors and engines, and he shifted to look out of the small circular window as the helicopter flew along the valley. He counted the dog-tags of his dead team in his pocket through the thick fabric of his combat trousers; one set was missing. As the helicopter flew close to the ground, he saw the two women he had shot, and for a moment the downwash lifted a rocket's parachute near to one of the women.

It might have just been a shadow or a trick of the light, but Grant thought he saw a young child looking up at him from under the parachute, but when he blinked, he was gone.

PART TWO

HER FUTURE, BECAUSE OF HIS PAST

CHAPTER NINETEEN
Cold House

The screen on the phone lit up, breaking the darkness in the room as the alarm sprung into life. Rachel reached out and jabbed at it to silence it but only succeeded to knock it to the floor where it went on beeping. Groaning, she leaned over to pick it up and squinted at the screen, which showed that it was 6.49 am. Rachel silenced the alarm then tossed it to one side and stayed lying on her bed, wondering if she could get away with a few more minutes of sleep.

Better not, too much to do.

Rachel rubbed her eyes and then stretched her arms out to the side and yawned noisily.

'Right then,' she declared, throwing back her covers and then shuffling towards the door to turn on the light. She stumbled across a pair of jeans and kicked them out of the way, knocking over an open can of cola which fizzed as it was absorbed into the carpet. Irritated, Rachel looked around for something to mop it up with and settled for using the Bon-Jovi t-shirt she had worn yesterday to rub at the liquid; the crucifix on her neck swaying as she did so. After a minute or so, she squatted back on her heels and considered the brown shape that the drink had formed in the dull grey carpet.

Looks a bit like the map of the world or something she thought.

She rolled the t-shirt up into a ball and tossed it to the corner of the room where it joined the mountain of clothes that she was growing there. The t-shirt hit the pile of clothes, uncurling slowly to show Jon Bon's crumpled face staring back at her, a dirty streak running over his cheek like a scar.

Sorry Jon, not sure whether you made it onto the clean pile or the dirty one.

She sat back on her bed and glanced around her room. There was just enough space for a bed, a closet, a set of ill-fitting drawers with a mirror on top and a narrow desk where Rachel avoided doing her studying. Next to the grimy window, photos of her friend Kim blended in with posters of her favourite bands and an Apocalypse Now poster proclaiming their love of the smell of Napalm. Rachel stared at them for a while and then she noticed the edge of her Karate certificate had peeled away from the wall. It was a long time since she had last trained, but she liked to see the certificate; she smoothed the surface of it and squashed the blu-tack back into the corner with her thumb. Her mother had forced her to take the classes to address her anger issues, Rachel hated doing the classes at first, but after a few sessions she enjoyed the training; not so much the Katas, but the actual sparring and splitting boards with her bare hands. Then out of the blue, her mother stopped letting her go,

twisting it around, saying that she had given up —
"something else you couldn't see through," she had told
her. Rachel didn't argue with her mother, she knew
better than that. She just went back upstairs, gently
closed the door to her room and stood crying in her
white uniform.

Rachel looked at herself in the mirror as she brushed
her brown hair and then touched the frayed edges of the
photograph taped to the corner of the mirror frame. It
was the only picture she had left of her father: her
mother had ripped up and burned the rest, but Rachel
had managed to save this one from the fire in the yard
when her mother went inside for more vodka. Rachel
thought he looked so handsome stood there in his best
uniform, in between two other men she didn't recognise
and whose names she had never known.

Wonder what he'd look like today?

Rachel suspected that her mother had other pictures
hidden somewhere, but no matter where she had looked,
she couldn't find any. Nothing, no wedding photos, no
pictures of her childhood, nothing. It was like she was
trying to forget her past — forget that she had even
existed in any other time than the present; or at the
bottom of a bottle. Rachel knew her father had been in
the Navy, she could tell by the smart blue uniform he
wore, but that was about all she knew. No matter how
insistent Rachel got, her mother wouldn't talk about
him, and they would often end up rowing for days. The
rows and the awkward silences she could handle, but
when her mother disappeared for days on end, leaving
her to look after her step-brother Josh, well that was an

entirely different matter. Before Josh was born, Rachel
had suspected that she was seeing somebody, although
she would never admit it, and the slightest suggestion
was enough to start the vicious circle of rows and
silences again. Rachel could remember her mother
sneaking a man into the house one night when she
thought she was asleep, but when her mother found out
she was pregnant with Josh, the men stopped coming,
and she stopped going out.

Rachel peeked through the curtains at the thick frost
clinging to car windscreens and the clean white snow
covering the pavements. Once the street woke up and set
about going to work and doing school runs, the roads
would become a dirty, slushy mess. Rachel didn't like
driving in snow and was glad that her mother would
drive them in today. Once dressed, she walked down the
corridor to knock on Josh's bedroom door, pausing a
moment before reaching in to find the light switch and
flick it on.

'Josh, it's time to get up.'

'No, five more minutes, please,' he replied sleepily.

'No, now, come on, I'll make you some breakfast after
I get mom up.'

Rachel waited until she heard Josh start to move then
she left the door ajar and walked down the corridor, past
their mother's room and down the stairs. The house was
cold, and the stairs creaked, breaking the silence as she
walked down into the living room. Rachel's mother was
asleep on the sofa holding an empty bottle of vodka on
her chest like a mother would cuddle a new-born baby.
Annoyed, Rachel kicked her mother's foot and told her

to get up.

'Come on mom you need to take Josh to school.'
There was no response, so she kicked again, harder this time.

'Stop it you bitch!'

'Get up and cut out that cussing, I don't want Josh to hear you talking like that.'

'I'll talk how I bloody well want to — it's my house you know.'

'Actually, its dad's house - Jesus, are you still drunk? Sort yourself out before Josh comes down.'

'Dad's house,' she snapped back at Rachel.

'Dad's house! It stopped being his house a long time ago, and that,' she said, pointing to Rachel's necklace, 'I've told you to stop wearing that piece of shit, if God existed, he'd give me a break from you. Wouldn't that be a miracle?'

Hearing Josh come noisily down the stairs, Rachel's mother sat up straight and hid the bottle behind the sofa.

'Hi Joshy, you okay little guy?' she said to him, her voice had a little slur.

'Yeah, I'm fine,' he replied, as he walked into the kitchen and sat at the table to wait for his breakfast.

'Make him some food would you Rachel - and a coffee for me.'

'Sure mom, anything for you,' Rachel said sarcastically.

Rachel ruffled Josh's short blond hair and fished out a spoon from the overflowing sink, rinsing it so he could eat his bowl of Corn Pops.

'Come on Josh, eat up we need to get going,' Rachel said, turning to look at her mother and seeing she had fallen back to sleep.

'Rachel?'

'What Josh?' she replied.

'Where's the dog, has she left him outside again?'

It wasn't the first time her mother had done this; let the dog out at night for him to do his business then forget to let him back in once her vodka kicked in. Rachel opened the door to look for him; the light spilling out of the kitchen revealed the dog curled up next to the trash can shivering.

'Cujo, come on boy. Come'

Cujo stood up slowly when he heard Rachel and half-heartedly wagged his tail. As with all German Shepherds of his age his back legs were wearing out, and he walked towards Rachel with a strange swagger which you might think was funny if you didn't know the reason for it. His head looked slightly wolfish, and despite his age, his eyes were alert, and he fixed them on Rachel as he lurched towards her. Despite being out all night, his coat still looked magnificent; a tawny yellow mass of long fur let down only by his white muzzle. On reaching Rachel, he sniffed her hand and looked up at her through cloudy eyes.

'Good boy Cujo, want some food?' She said, as she eased the door shut behind him.

Rachel stroked him as she tipped kibble into his bowl and he nibbled at it with a lazy lacklustre.

Out of nowhere, Josh said quietly, 'Rachel, is mom sick?'

Yes, she is, but it's her own damn fault she wanted to say.

Rachel bit her lip, 'no Josh, she's just a bit tired, are you ready to go? C' mon, I'll walk you to the bus stop.'

'I thought mom would drive us today,' replied Josh, dragging his favourite green and white scarf behind him.

'Maybe tomorrow, we'll get the bus today. Come on, put your coat on and let's go.'

Their mother didn't stir as they walked past her to leave the house. The chill air outside caused their breath to steam and Josh delighted in letting out long breaths through his nostrils. Despite the cold, Rachel was enjoying chatting to her younger brother who was telling her about his day ahead and the complex politics of the 5th grade. But they had only walked a short distance when Josh realised that he had forgotten his backpack, so they turned around and hurried back to their house.

'Just wait out here Josh, I won't be a minute.'

'Okay,' said Josh as he wrote his name in the snow on their porch with his foot.

'My bags under the table I think,' he added as Rachel went back into the house.

Rachel paused when she got to the living room, the sofa was empty, but the television was on, and the channel was showing an advert for the latest must-have fitness device that could be paid for in three convenient instalments.

Stupid bitch must have gone to bed now it's time to get up, I need to do something about her.

Rachel picked up the backpack from under the table, and as she turned around, her mother grabbed her by the throat and pinned her up against the refrigerator. She could smell alcohol and vomit and something else that she couldn't quite make out on her mother's breath. Rachel tried to push her away, but she was bigger and heavier, and the grip on her throat tightened.

'What are you doing you crazy bitch?' Rachel managed to say. There was rage in her mother's eyes, much more anger than the last time she did this. Cujo growled a warning, unsure what to do and whose side he should take. Rachel felt sharp fingernails cutting into her skin. She dropped the backpack and pushed on her mother's chin to force her head back, she resisted but finally let go and took a step back. They stared at each other for a long moment and then Rachel reached down to pick up the backpack, not taking her eyes off her mother. She couldn't feel it near to her feet, so she looked down to see where it was. This was when her mother saw her chance, slapping her hard across the face, nearly forcing her to her knees. Cujo barked and bared his yellowed teeth and looked from one to the other still unsure of whose side to take.

Seconds later, the door opened, and Josh shouted, 'what's going on? Come on Rachel we need to go, my teacher said we could make snow angels if it snowed last night. And it did snow a lot, Rachel, come on already!'

Rachel pressed her hand over her cheek, it stung when she touched it, and she hoped that it wouldn't swell up and bruise.

'Nothing Josh, coming now,' she said as she turned and left the house. Hiding her tears, she took hold of her brother's hand and walked him to the bus stop as if nothing had happened.

CHAPTER TWENTY

Fast Friends

Josh's school bus turned up late due to the driver having to take her time in the icy conditions. Rachel waited and watched Josh as he grinned at her through the steamed up window of the yellow bus until it turned the corner. It was a ten-minute walk from the bus stop to college and she had already missed the start of the first period, so Rachel took her time, no point rushing now. Her feet made crunching noises as she walked through crisp patches of snow on the sidewalk and she enjoyed herself despite the bitter cold biting at her cheeks. She winced as a blast of sleet stung her face as if her mother had slapped her again. As she walked, Rachel texted her friend Kim telling her where to meet her and smiled despite being swore at after bumping into an old man walking his scruffy looking Scottie dog. The man had a weather-beaten face and his white stubble matched the colour of the dog's whiskers and off-white coloured paws. He growled something offensive and then turned his collar up at the back, so it met the thick woollen hat he had pulled down to cover the tips of his ears. The dog looked at Rachel through almost closed eyes as it cocked its leg by a fire hydrant; if it was possible for animals to look pissed off, this one certainly did apparently not enjoying his walk in the cold this morning. The dogs back leg shook as he balanced while he turned the snow and his paws yellow. The clean smelling air changed as she passed them to something sweet like smoking wood, almost earthy tasting as she breathed in his second-hand cigarette smoke.

Before she knew it, Rachel had arrived at college on auto-pilot without remembering the rest of the walk. She collected her late pass from the disapproving receptionist who then went back to her crossword puzzle and waited in the corridor by her locker for Kim. Rachel and Kim had been the best of friends since being forced to solve a math problem in Mrs Colley's 6th Grade class. They didn't like each other at first; Rachel thought Kim was aloof and Kim didn't like the look of Rachel with her neat hair and perfect teeth, but Mrs Colley had not been in a good mood and they thought better of causing a fuss. And so, through solving the mysteries of algebra they became fast friends and became inseparable ever since.

Rachel and Kim both had medium brown coloured hair which they often wore in similar styles. They were roughly the same height, but Kim had a fuller figure, perhaps harshly described as a little plump. This had not stopped the unwanted attention of boys over the years, and although she had plenty of offers, Kim had never wanted a boyfriend. In stark contrast, Rachel was proud that she was the first girl to have a boyfriend, almost from the moment she set foot in high school. Kim thought boys were nothing but trouble, based on the amount of Ben and Jerry's she had to use on a regular basis to drag her friend out of post break up wallowing and despair.

The heating had been cranked up, making the classroom far too hot and humid. Even the flagpole in the corner seemed to struggle to hold up its faded star-spangled companion. It was one of those lessons that seemed to cause time to stand still and Rachel was sure she could hear gentle snoring coming from somewhere in the room. The girls were counting down the time to the end of the last lesson of the day, even Kim was looking bored, and she loved learning — a real 'try-hard' as Rachel often teased her. Rachel looked at Kim with mischief in her eyes faking a long yawn while nodding towards the clock above the whiteboard that their teacher scribbled on. The squeaky noise that the pen made as he dragged it back and forth on the board as he wrote was surprisingly loud. Perhaps even he had had enough of his own voice today and needed something to keep himself going. The noise did, however, seem to stop the snoring; or perhaps the snorer's body clock had evolved over the years spent in school and had adapted to awaken them refreshed moments before the lecture was due to end. Rachel looked at Kim and rolled her eyes before shifting in her seat to see if she could find out who was lucky enough to have been able to sleep through some of today's lesson. As usual, Steve Flint

stared back at her with hope in his bright green eyes and
a promise in his smile. Rachel smiled back and thought
on this for a moment before turning away, feeling
slightly embarrassed.

After a moment she glanced back, studying his face
and watching the way that his hand moved gracefully
over the page. He looked up and smiled again, the
kindness in it alarming her.

Steven bloody Flint. He's a computing major, so he is
kind of smart, but he's not really my type.

But… well, does that matter anyway?

She smiled back in a 'maybe, maybe not' way hoping
that it would have the desired effect.

Did he blush? That's so adorable. Palm of my hand
Stevie boy, palm of my hand.

The teacher babbled on about something he thought
was essential for them to know, but Rachel's attention
was now firmly elsewhere. Kim tapped her on the
shoulder and gestured for her to pay attention to what
the teacher was saying.

'Try hard!' she whispered with a broad smile.

'Excuse me, ladies. Is there a problem?' said the
teacher, who couldn't pronounce his 'r's.

'No, there's no ploblem,' they replied almost in
tandem.

'Mm,' he muttered not sure if they were making fun of
him, fixing them both with his death stare which went on
for a little too long. The uncomfortable silence was
savoured by everyone else in the room except the girls.
The bell broke the tension with its loud rattle, causing
the classroom to erupt into a rowdy free for all as bags

were hurriedly packed as everybody headed for the door like a pack of wildebeests who had spotted a way to escape from a predator.

'Remember! I need your essay immediately after the break for extra credit!' the teacher barked over the noise.

'Come on Kim, hurry up,' said Rachel.

'All right already,' replied Kim, feeling a little uncomfortable as she watched Steve ease past Rachel a little too close for her liking. Rachel didn't seem to mind, though, and she even pushed her hips forward ever so slightly as he passed.

Kim wasn't the only person who noticed. Sat in the back corner was a thin, dark-haired boy called Kyle who was staring at Rachel with an odd look of concern on his face. Kyle was a quiet boy that nobody seemed to take any notice of, yet Rachel felt his stare and turned to face him. His expression did not change. Rachel expressed her feelings toward him with her middle finger.

'What's your problem, asshole?'

Nothing, no reply.

'Are you fucking deaf or something? I asked you if you have a fucking problem.'

The teacher's selective deafness kicked in as he headed out of the door, scurrying home to begin his week of freedom and ready meals, leaving the three of them alone in the room.

'Come on, Rachel, take no notice. Let's go,' Kim urged, packing up the rest of her friends books into her bag and then pulling on her arm, leading Rachel towards the door. Kyle's gaze never left the girls and followed them all the way out of the room. He continued looking at the empty doorway for several minutes before he carefully packed his books away and stood up. He moved over to Rachel's desk, knelt down, and pressed his nose into her seat and inhaled deeply. Kyle was a quiet boy, the sort of boy that nobody seemed to take any notice of.

CHAPTER TWENTY-ONE

7

God saw how great the wickedness of the human race had become on the earth, and that every inclination of the thoughts of the human heart was only evil all the time.

What a glorious time to be alive.

CHAPTER TWENTY-TWO

Love Locked

The corridors were noisy and chaotic. Students struggled to get to their lockers, or to their friends, or just to the nearest way out of the building. There was a happy buzz in the air, and everybody was in high spirits looking forward to a welcome break from school. The girls skilfully navigated past the various groups you find in any college or high school. The 'it' girls, too busy to acknowledge anyone outside their circle as they bitched on about somebody; the jocks in their baseball jackets checking out the 'it' girls; the pale white Goth's, who never seemed to smile or look at anybody; the geeks excitedly talking about how they can't wait to try the latest piece of software; the cheerleaders and the loners. As they walked, Kim looked at Rachel through the corner of her eyes.

I wonder what group we belong in, she thought. Rachel could have been an 'it' girl, she is pretty enough for them. A geek? No, I don't think so, she hates studying with a passion. She could have carried on being a cheerleader though if she hadn't lost her temper and tried to tell the coach how to do her job. Anyway, cheerleaders are way too perky all the time, they must be on some sort of drug to keep that up all the time.

Kim let out a little giggle as she imagined Rachel dressed as a Goth.

'What's up?'

'Oh, nothing,' she smiled.

'What?'

'Okay then - I was just imagining you as a Goth,' replied Kim.

'Me dressed up like one of those freaks, I don't think so,' then, frowning she added, 'although I do look great in black, don't I?'

You look great in anything...

'Come on Kim we're nearly at our lockers, what do you think you'll get in the yearbook? Best student? Teacher's pet? The student most likely to become a millionaire. What do you reckon?'

'Oh, I don't know, I don't really care about that stuff.' Kim said.

'Well, what about me? What will I get, most likely to marry for money? Or, I know... most likely to become a nun?'

Kim looked at her with raised eyebrows and said, 'you a nun, seriously?' The biggest flirt more like...

'No, I can't see me as a nun either Kim - I'd find it hard to break the habit. Do you get it? Habit?'

Kim groaned, 'yeah, I get it.'

On a roll now Rachel said, 'hey Kim, what do you call a nun who walks in her sleep?'

'I don't know, why don't you tell me?'

'A roaming catholic,' said Rachel with a deadpan expression.

'That's terrible Rachel, really terrible, even for you.' Said Kim, who couldn't help giggling. Rachel laughed as she turned to Kim and said, 'Okay then, most likely to be a stand-up comedian, that's what they will give me.'

I love the way your nose wrinkles when you smile...

When they reached their lockers, Kim spun the combination of the lock, took out two textbooks and shoved them into her bag.

'Seriously Kim, it's the holidays, loosen up a little.' Rachel said, raising her eyebrows.

'Just because it's the holidays doesn't mean you should stop studying, you know.'

'Screw that,' Rachel said, opening her locker, tossing her books in it into it and slamming it shut. Kim waited until she was sure Rachel wasn't looking before reaching back into her own locker for a heart-shaped padlock which she slipped into her pocket.

As they left the building and walked down the wide concrete steps, Kim looked up at the drab grey sky, the clouds slowly swirling like oily rags.

'We'd better hurry up — looks like snow again,' she said, then added, 'you know Rachel, I expect we'll miss this place when we leave.'

'This place,' Rachel replied with her arms spread wide, 'is a dump Kim - you can't be serious.'

A little put out by the comment, Kim walked along in silence until they arrived at the bridge that led over the Charles River to Centre Street. Kim looked over to the circular buildings of MIT in the distance, wondering when they would send her acceptance letter. Or perhaps it would be a refusal letter she thought, as the top of MIT disappeared as a thick mist began to fall covering its slender domes.

Rachel brushed her fingers over the chain-link fence and splashed her feet in the slushy mess of snow that had built up on the sidewalk. For almost the entire length of the bridge, a chain-link fence stretched along on top of a waist-high wall. The fence had been put up following a suicide one year, and despite its association with death, it was known locally as the Love Bridge. A pretty young fifteen-year-old girl called Scarlet Hanson had left home one Christmas Day to throw herself off the bridge into the freezing water. Initially, the reason for her suicide was unknown; she was tall, beautiful and amazingly bright with a world of opportunity ahead of her.

Immediately after seeing her daughter lowered into the cold earth, her mother went to the exact spot that her daughter had leapt from. The incident had understandably attracted a lot of media coverage, and the press had followed her to the bridge, their cameras clicking away like vultures picking at the bones of a corpse. Scarlet's mother took out a lock which had their names on it and locked it on to the fence above the water that had taken her daughter's life. She wore the key on a chain close to her heart to symbolise their eternal love. Nobody can fully understand the pain caused by burying a child, it's something people never truly get over, but things soon got worse however when Scarlet's mother found a set of diaries graphically describing the terrible abuse that her husband had subjected their daughter to over several years. She plunged a kitchen knife deep into his chest while he was asleep, and the police erected the fence soon after in case the area turned into an attraction for copycats and people who might get off on that sort of thing. The husband was discovered weeks later when a neighbour noticed they had not seen him or his wife for a while, and a peculiar odour could be smelled through the walls. The police found the husbands corpse surrounded by the diaries; the Hansen's joint bank account was empty, and the wife was never heard from again. Rumours were that she had fled to Europe and it was rumoured that the police hadn't searched particularly hard to locate her.

People had either forgotten, or more likely no longer cared about the sad history resulting in the fence being erected, and it was now covered in locks of all shapes and sizes forming a multicoloured patchwork of undying love. There was a pile of bricks and some scaffolding at the far end of the bridge where construction workers had begun to repair a damaged part of the wall before the bad weather had stopped them. The girls had to walk on the road to get past a coned off area. Rachel could see the river through the missing section of the wall, and she shivered as she thought about the girl ending her life in the icy water. She had heard of people surviving falling through ice as the body's survival system set in and reflexes closed the throat to prevent water from entering the lungs, but unfortunately this hadn't happened to Scarlet.

Then again, Rachel thought, she probably didn't want it to.

Her dark thoughts were interrupted by Kim when she said, 'Rach, look at the locks, look how pretty they are when the light catches the frost on them.'

Rachel regarded her with a quizzical expression, 'Kim, you know for someone who has never had a boyfriend you certainly are a romantic.'

Kim felt her cheeks flush and was about to say something when Rachel added, 'but it's all bullshit, you know, love, romance, these locks, everything is bullshit. You think boys are romantic? Romantic my ass. Romance - is that what you call it? Is that what it is until they've got what they wanted from you? And these love locks - I bet there are a few couples who wish they'd kept spare keys.'

The girls were over the bridge now and turned to walk down Centre Street towards the Ladder 25 Fire Station.

'Well, would you look at that,' said Rachel, as she linked arms with Kim, bumping hips, almost forcing her into the road as she nodded towards the firefighters washing the grime from the front of their fire engine.

'Oh, it looks like they could be in a diet coke advert if only they took their winter clothes off. Shall we ask them to Kim?' Rachel teased.

'Don't you dare!' said Kim, brushing flakes of snow from her friend's shoulder.

'Come on Kim, maybe one would make a perfect boyfriend for you - you have to take the plunge one day you know.'

'Please don't Rachel, don't,' Kim said, as they got

closer to the fire station. Sparing Kim's embarrassment, Rachel said nothing to the firefighters but just burst out laughing. The firefighters looked up, taking the opportunity for a brief rest from their mundane task. Kim couldn't help laughing herself, and when she noticed Rachel smiling at her, she felt her heartbeat quicken in response.

They stopped at the end of the block near to the public library, and Rachel put her hands on Kim's shoulders and looked at her.

'Look, Kim, its Halloween in a few months, let's do all the touristy stuff so we can remember what Boston is like while we still have the chance. You know before you go off to your fancy university and I start flipping burgers somewhere.'

'Don't say that Rachel, you'll get great grades and a good job if you focus a little more.'

They looked into each other's eyes for a long moment before Kim broke the silence between them.

'Alright, it's a date, but I'm not getting dressed up, it took me ages to get that fake blood off my hands last time — it was worse than one of your fake tanning sessions. Well, almost as bad.'

'We'll see Kim — you know I always get my way in the end, don't I.' Rachel said with a wry smile.
Kim looked up and down the street at the drab buildings.

'Anyway Rach, what are you doing tomorrow?'

'Oh, the usual start to the weekend I expect, me and Josh will sleep in late while mom goes shopping, then I'll play with Josh, Cowboys and Indians usually. That's what he's into at the moment.

Right 'I'll message you later — need to run now to

meet Josh at his bus stop,' Rachel said hugging Kim before they set off in different directions to make their way back home.

Kim turned around and waited for a while with her hands in her pockets, savouring the sway of Rachel's hips as she walked away.

When she was sure Rachel was out of sight, Kim took the padlock out of her pocket and looked at the engraving of a heart encircled with her and Rachel's names.

CHAPTER TWENTY-THREE
Ctrl Alt Delete

It was already growing dark by the time Rachel and Josh
arrived home from the bus stop and a thin blanket of
snow already coated the road and the top of parked cars.
Josh ran ahead and pulled off his glove so he could
scrape his name and a smiley face into the ice on the rear
window of a car parked outside their house. The 'tongue
face' he called the faces whenever he drew one as they
always had a tongue spilling out from a fat-lipped
mouth.

'That's a good one Josh,' Rachel said as she reached
the car.

Rachel fully expected her mother to continue the fight
from earlier, so she encouraged Josh to draw more
shapes on the window as she didn't want him to hear
them argue. She walked up the steps to her house,
pausing on the narrow wooden porch and looked down
at the scruffy 'welcome' mat laid out in front of the
door. It didn't really offer a welcome in its muddy wet
state, and they never had many visitors to welcome

anyway. After a quick glance back at Josh, who smiled at her as he got back to crafting his shapes, Rachel slid her key into the lock. As she began to turn it, the door swung open with a disapproving groan. The door didn't always lock properly after it had been broken after being slammed shut once.

Rachel recalled that particular argument; nothing specific about what she had said to start it, but the sight of her mother rushing towards her in a frenzied state was still remarkably vivid. She remembered being thrown out of the house and tripping over the mat, falling headfirst down the steps and breaking her wrist. Her mother thought she was putting it on and called her an attention-seeking bitch and ranted on about how Rachel never gave her a minute's peace, but when a neighbour got social services involved, she soon changed her tune. Rachel sat quietly through the meetings where her mother convinced the dour-faced social workers that she was a fit mother and she knew what was best for her child. Rachel had often wondered why her mother hadn't just let them take her away, she always said she wanted to be rid of her. Perhaps Rachel was getting it wrong, after all, she was only seven years old at the time.

Apprehensively, Rachel entered the house, her fingers tracing lightly over the wall, automatically finding the light switch. She paused in the doorway warily looking out for her mother and was surprised to see that the house was reasonably clean, and a pair of defrosting Mac & Jack ready meals had been left out next to the microwave. Cujo looked up contentedly from his basket under the dinner table, apparently well-fed, his fur looked smooth and silky after being brushed. The house seemed quiet and still until Josh ran in banging the door shut behind him, causing Rachel to jump. Josh trudged into the kitchen, leaving a trail of wet slushy footprints on the carpet as he went over to stroke the dog.

Josh quickly polished off his own meal and was happily tucking into Rachel's which they had eaten straight out the cartons to save on washing up. Rachel stood up was about to draw the kitchen window curtains when the front door opened, and their mother appeared.

'Mom?' Rachel called out.

'Hi guy's,' she hesitated, one foot on the bottom stair, 'I've got a bit of a headache, so I'm off to bed,' she announced as she walked up them.

'Night,' she shouted back down before closing her bedroom door. Josh looked quizzically at Rachel, who shrugged her shoulders in response.

'Bipolar,' Rachel whispered to herself.

'What did you say Rach?'

'Oh, nothing Josh — just thinking aloud, come on now give me a hug then get yourself ready for bed.'

For once Josh didn't stall for extra time. He kicked off his shoes by the front door leaving a new black mark on the wall and wearily headed up the stairs, worn out after playing in the snow all day at school.

'Wash your face and brush your teeth,' Rachel reminded him, accepting his groan as confirmation.

Rachel changed into her pyjamas then lay down on her bed, skimming through the emails on her laptop that she had balanced precariously on one knee. The semi-normality of the evening had put her in a good mood, and she was enjoying holding the delete key down getting rid of the spam and numerous requests from her tutors for overdue work. She was halfway through typing an email to her English Lit teacher asking for another extension to her existing extension, when her phone on the table buzzed as a text message arrived. Happy to get a break from trying to come up with a valid excuse, Rachel stood up, setting her laptop on the table opposite the bed as she reached for the phone. Through the scratched screen, she saw.

NEW MESSAGE FROM UNKNOWN

Curious, Rachel unlocked the phone to discover that the message had come from Steve.

'What R U doing?' the message asked.

'None of your business,' she messaged back, looking at the phone and smiling.

Almost immediately, he messaged her again.

'But it could be…'

'Maybe, I'll think about it. Don't text again I'm going to bed now,' Rachel sent.

'Bedtime. Sounds good, can I come?'

Rachel quickly typed out a reply on her phone and then paused before pressing send. Smiling, she deleted it and sent, 'Goodnight!'

She waited, a little disappointed that no response came back this time, so she climbed into bed after plugging the charger into the phone. Rachel waited a moment for the "This accessory is not supported on this device" warning to disappear before putting the phone on the floor next to her bed. She was just about to fall asleep when the phone buzzed again.

NEW MESSAGE FROM UNKNOWN

He is persistent, I'll give him that.

The message said, 'can't sleep sent u an email.'

Rachel opened the laptop screen and logged back into her email account. In the Inbox was a message from Steve_F.

Let's see what's on your mind then Steve underscore F, Rachel thought as she clicked on the email to open it. It was empty.

OKAY, then nothing in here — must be in the attachment. Rachel clicked on the paperclip shape of the attachment, which caused the screen to flicker, but the attachment didn't open. She clicked it once more, but the same thing happened.

'Asshole,' she said out loud, frustratedly stabbing at the power button to switch off the laptop before clambering back into bed.

How did he get my phone number anyway? She wondered as she settled down under her duvet. The room was already getting cold but it the warmth in her bed drew her closer to sleep. The only light in the room came from the screen of her laptop, which hadn't properly turned off. She should really get up to close the lid, but it didn't matter as the screen would dim soon when battery saving mode kicked in, and well, the bed was far too comfy to leave.

After a short while, the screen faded to black and Rachel finally succumbed to sleep. An hour later, the small red light next to her webcam lit up and started a live recording.

CHAPTER TWENTY-FOUR
Outline of Mine

Kim gently closed the lid of her laptop and smiled. When she remembered how much money she needed to pay back to her parents, her smile soon faded. She'd probably have to get a job busing tables in a diner for a few months, but it would all be worth it if she got into MIT. On an open morning tour of the MIT campus, Kim had seen a post-grad student offering a confidential essay writing service. She was curious to see how skilled a writer she might become if she made it to MIT, so she had sent them some of her homework tasks as a test. The work was so good that her teachers were suspicious of her at first as she had moved from a B-minus to an A-plus virtually overnight. However, under pressure from above to get good results, the teachers turned a blind eye to it, although they all knew it wasn't her work. Some of the tests in class were a bit tricky, but Kim managed to convince everybody that her poor performances were down to nerves, and she soon accumulated enough credit to apply for a place in MIT.

Kim got up from her bed and went to the window to peer out into the rear garden at the trees heavy with snow. Even in winter, they seemed to keep most of their leaves, and in the moonlight, they reminded Kim of the trees you would see on a cheap Christmas card, the sort that Rachel would send you. Kim had a large room which took up a corner aspect of the house. It was over twice the size of Rachel's cramped, messy room; one window looked out onto the street and the other directly into her rear garden.

She liked where she lived, it wasn't the tree-lined white picket fence type of street, but it was as close as you could get without moving out of Boston altogether. It was certainly a nicer place to live than where Rachel's house was, where it must be so annoying having cars rushing past all the time. Kim's parents had cut out the middleman and brought the house at a reasonable price directly from the builders who were sliding rapidly towards bankruptcy. It was clad in light blue wood in the traditional colonial style complete with painted white slatted shutters and was by far the biggest house on the street. It backed onto a small unkempt wood who nobody knew owned which Kim used to be scared of venturing into in the daytime, let alone at night, but as she grew older, she spent more time in there getting to know where the spiderweb of trails led to. If she was late for college, she could walk through the woods to cut ten minutes from her journey time and pop out just a couple of blocks away from Rachel's house.

The only light in the room came from the small lamp beside her bed, and as moved across to the window to look out to the street, her body cast a very pleasing silhouette. She caught sight of the teenage boy staring into her bedroom again from his room across the street as he often did. Kim had never acknowledged this or challenged him about it. Kim had seen him in his room tonight, his curtains slightly open, but his room was completely dark. She knew he would be watching; she wanted him to. Boys were not her thing, but she enjoyed the power that her body seemed to have over them. Kim slowly stripped to her underwear and waited for a long moment before closing the curtains and turning off the light. From outside, it looked like she'd gone to bed.

Shortly after, Kim got dressed in the dark into a black tracksuit, pulled on a black baseball cap and went downstairs to her living room where her father sat slumped in his favourite chair watching a re-run of a Red-Sox game as her mother slept fitfully on the sofa.

'Where are you going at this time of night?' he asked in a broad Boston accent.

Kim looked at the beer bottle he rested on his ample stomach as she laced up her sneakers, 'nowhere, just going for a quick run around the block.'

'Sure, but why can't you go at a normal time. You know, like in the daytime, like a normal person.' He said without looking away from the television screen; it was one of his favourite games although he had never been to see a live match at the 'Green Monsta.'

'I just prefer it at this time of night; there's no-one around.'

He gulped beer from the bottle, spilling a drop on his white vest, 'you don't know who is around at…' he began.

'Leave her alone,' her mother said sleepily. 'Stick to the streets Kim where they're well lit. Take your phone and don't be too long.'

'I won't mom, I'll be back before you know it,' Kim said as she walked through the house into the kitchen to leave via the side door. She overheard her mother say, 'leave her alone Dan, you know she's self-conscious about her weight,' as she carefully closed the door.

Thanks, mom, you bitch.

Kim zipped up her tracksuit to keep out the light snow and jogged slowly down the street, keeping an eye on the boy's window across the street. Checking that his curtains were closed, and he wasn't watching her, she turned and ran back to her house. If anybody else saw her they would just think she'd changed her mind about going for a run in the snow; as far as the teenage peeping Tom was concerned she was still in the house; both useful alibis.

She strolled back to her front door and listened to the presenter on the television starting the countdown to the best ever Red-Sox player, but instead of going in, she crept around to the rear of her house and ran carefully across the garden then clambered clumsily over the fence into the woods. On the other side, Kim stood for a minute, letting her eyes adjust to the blackness. Despite spending months planning for tonight, as she stood there in the dark, she found herself having second thoughts.

She turned around and placed her hands on the fence to climb back over, but she hesitated when she saw her father's body briefly illuminated by the light of the refrigerator as he pulled out another bottle. The strip light in the kitchen fluttered on and her mother trudged in wearily, cigarette already in mouth and began making a sandwich. Kim slid down and pressed her back against the fence. There was no turning back now.

Despite the cold she was already sweating as she set off, following the trail skirting around the edge of the woods as she had done so many times before. When she arrived at the chain-link fence at the boundary of the woods, she followed it around to the corner where the fence continued at a right angle. Kim paused there, listening to see if anybody else was in the woods, but she couldn't hear anything over the pounding of her heart. Sweat stung her eyes as she knelt down and searched for the small pile of rocks she had set down the day before on her way into college. Her fingers found the object she had buried, and she stood still, clutching it to her chest. It took a moment to gather the courage to remove it from the plastic bag, and the metal seemed to absorb the faint light when she looked down at it. Kim walked on more slowly now until she reached the gap in the fence that she'd used a set of her father's pliers to cut months ago. As she pushed through the hole, the cuff of her tracksuit became snagged on the fence, and as she yanked her arm free, the rusty fence snapped back cutting into the back of her hand.

Kim ran on ignoring the pain, and within ten minutes, she was standing outside Rachel's house with the knife in her hand.

CHAPTER TWENTY-FIVE

6

I can feel their breath close to my face. It is always there, constant, in and out. In and out all the time. It's like a gentle whisper peaceful and reassuring. I think I am safe as long as I hear that noise. I don't believe in God. At least I don't think I do. Or do I? Have I ever? I can't remember anymore. Perhaps I should, maybe that way I will wake up. Why can't I wake up? Perhaps I am in purgatory waiting to be judged. Well, if I am what are you waiting for God? When will you decide on my fate? Oh, what if we have all got it wrong, and it isn't you that decides. Is it the red bastard who really has the power to decide? Okay then Satan, what do I have to do to get out of here? Come on, I'm asking you. What do I have to do?

I listen carefully for a response. Nothing, nothing except for the breath. Always the breath. In and out, constant, reassuring. And then I hear them whisper, 'She knows what she has to do.'

CHAPTER TWENTY-SIX

8 Tracks

Rachel woke early the next day. Her mother had switched the heating on making the house uncharacteristically hot, and she wasn't used to the warmth. Rachel heard voices downstairs, so she kicked her duvet off the bed, put on yesterday's clothes and went downstairs. Her mother and Josh were sat at the table, happily chattering away.

'Coffee Rachel?', her mom suggested.

'Okay… sure, that'd be great,' she replied, confused at the sudden introduction of normality.

'I'll make it, let me, let me,' Josh said excitedly, as he slid awkwardly off his stool.

'Be careful,' Rachel and her mother said almost in unison, and they couldn't help smiling at each other.

'I will — course I will, I know how to do it,' he considered both of them in turn, 'I'm not a baby you know,' he declared, grabbing hold of the coffeepot and pouring too much into a cup causing the hot brown liquid to spill over onto the table.

Rachel rushed for a towel to clean it up well aware that

her mother had become angry over much less in the past.

'I've got it,' her mother said, 'you sit down and enjoy your coffee, Rachel.'

She glanced at the window. 'It's still snowing, so me and Josh are just going to nip out to pick up a few groceries before the snow really comes down — do you want anything in particular?'

'No, I'm good. No, actually could you pick me up some cotton wool. You know the makeup removal pads, the circular ones?' Rachel replied.

'Sure, no problem. Ready to get going Josh, we'll go over the padlock bridge if you like?' Her mom suggested.

'Yep, let's go,' Josh said, putting his coat on as he headed toward the door.

Rachel grabbed his arm and whirled him around, 'forgetting something are we Josh?' She said, standing with her arms wide open for a hug.

'No what? Oh — okaayyyy then,' he said, as he rushed up to Rachel and squeezed her tight. Rachel kissed the top of his head and pulled up his zipper, tucking his scarf in snuggly around his neck, then spun him around and pushed him gently towards the door.

'Off you go, have fun.'

Rachel followed them out and waited on the porch, arms folded around herself against the cold as she watched them climb into the car. The snow had fallen steadily overnight and, despite it being only mid-morning, the sky was dark with heavy clouds stalking overhead threatening to burst at any moment. The wheels spun quickly in the snow until they made contact with the road and with a lurch, the car pulled away. Rachel noticed a narrow strip of thawed ice under the car, probably just an oil leak and as the car started down the street it left behind a thin trail of liquid behind. The greenish liquid dotted the snow reminding her of Hansel and Gretel, leaving breadcrumbs so they could find their way back home. She saw Josh appear in the rear window as he knelt up on the rear seat waving goodbye to Rachel with a big broad smile on his face.

Rachel mouthed, 'seatbelt, put your seatbelt on,' and Josh mimicked her fasten seatbelt hand movements. He was still looking at her as the car drove further away and continued waving until it disappeared around the corner.

As Rachel turned to go back into the house, she saw another car pull away from the opposite side of the street and head off in the same direction that her mother had gone. The driver glanced over at Rachel through his misty window and held her gaze as he passed. He appeared to say something, and his car sped up, and it soon disappeared around the corner. Rachel walked back into her house and pushed the door shut and then it began to snow hard, big fat flakes falling rapidly to settle on the pavement.

Rachel's mother looked at Josh in the rear-view mirror as he knelt waving at back at Rachel.

'Josh, sit down!' she shouted to him as she tried to eject the cassette from the stereo. Josh sometimes played in the car when his mom had been sleepy and fallen asleep on the sofa, and he had jammed a tape into the slot upside down once, and now the eject button didn't always work. The heater was on full blast, making the car hot, but the blowers struggled to clear the mist from the inside of the windscreen. Rachel's mother leaned forward to wipe the glass with the back of her hand, which only seemed to make it worse. As she swung onto the Love Bridge, the combination of smeared water on the inside of the windscreen and the rapid snowfall made it very hard to see. The rear lights of the cars in front disappeared now and again in the thickening snowstorm.

With one eye on the road ahead Rachel's mother fumbled with the stereo again, jabbing at the eject button frantically.

'Can't see the padlocks,' Josh stated.

'What?'

'Should have listened to Rachel,' Josh said helpfully from behind her, 'and gotten a CD player, then this wouldn't have happened, would it? If you bought a modern car, it would have a CD player already, wouldn't it? Can we have a new car mom, how old is this car anyway? My friend, Daniel Wright's car, has buttons you press that make the windows open, not like ours that we have to wind down. And it has a CD player'.

'Yes Josh,' she said wearily, as she repeatedly pressed the eject button until the cassette flew out leaving behind a trail of brown tape stuck in the stereo.

'Shit!' she said as she tugged at the damaged tape and threw it onto the passenger seat.

'Josh, I've told you to sit down!'

'OKAY, mom.'

'I think it's all out now,' she said, pulling out the last of the thin brown tape.

'So, Josh, do you want Meatloaf or Bonnie Tyler?'

Josh groaned, 'can't we just have the radio on? My friend Daniel...' he began, but his mother cut him off swiftly, 'no you know it doesn't work after the aerial broke off in the car wash, remember?'

Despite the heavy snowfall, traffic was moving fast, too fast. Perhaps everybody wanted to get their chores done quickly and get back to the warmth of their homes. The windscreen wipers were on full now, the frozen rubber thudding and shuddering over the part-frozen windscreen. As soon as they cleared the screen, it was covered again. She pulled on the lever to spray screen wash to melt the snow, but none came, it was either frozen or empty. Snow was building up on the bottom of the windscreen now and was blocking them from returning fully to the start position. Rachel's mother didn't seem to notice. With each passing moment, the effectiveness of the wipers was decreasing millimetres at a time. She reached over to the glove compartment to find a new cassette.

'Where are you Bonnie Tyler?' she sang out loud over the thrum of the wipers. Without looking away from the road, she fished around in the glove compartment until she found a tape and held it up to look at the label printed on it, but the car hit a pothole, and it slipped out of her hand and landed between her feet.

'Damn you Bonnie, you bitch!' She was not singing now.

She looked down, the tape had fallen underneath the pedals and was out of her reach, she'd have to get it when she stopped if it wasn't crushed by her feet by then.

'Okay then, no stupid bitch Bonnie - what else have we got?'

She glanced sideways to look for another tape, and this was when she saw the metallic glint of the handgun.

'What the hell!'

'What's up mom?'

'Nothing Josh, it's fine,' she replied, slamming the glove compartment shut.

CHAPTER TWENTY-SEVEN

Muddy Puddles

The car rocked as if something had hit them from behind, then a fraction of a second later a loud rattling noise came from underneath the rear of the vehicle. Before they knew what was happening, they had swerved into the opposite lane. Rachel's mother tugged on the steering wheel, but on the icy road, the tyres fought to grip, and there was barely any control. Eventually, the tyres gained some purchase, and at the last moment, they narrowly missed the car coming straight towards them. She jabbed at the brake pedal; it felt like she was pressing down onto a sponge; it did nothing to slow the car down. Josh screamed as the side of the car scraped along the crash barrier; bright sparks spurting high into the air as metal met metal. The metal barrier was the only thing stopping them from mounting the sidewalk. Part of the crash barrier caught in the rim of the rear wheel and dug into the tyre causing rubber fragments to fly out in all directions, black slashes in the snow. Fractions of a second later the tyre lost its air and shredded. The stench of hot wet rubber flooding in from the air vents was oppressive. The car slid into the onrushing traffic again. Panic set in as she yanked the wheel back, making the front wheels shift slightly. The car met the crash barrier again, so she kept the steering wheel locked tight to slow the car down by scrapping it along the metal. She couldn't see it through the snowfall, but she had just made the car head for the gap in the wall and the twenty-foot drop to the freezing river below. The car clattered into the scaffolding then time seemed to slow as the vehicle left the bridge. It was strangely quiet with the road no longer beneath the car to dampen its noise; the engine sounded oddly beautiful. The car smashed into the frozen riverbank side on, crumpling the bonnet and a jagged crack appeared across the windscreen.

Despite gripping tightly, the shock of the impact caused Rachel's mother's hands to fly off the steering wheel. The back of her right hand struck the gear stick, breaking bones, her left hand flew into her face in an absurd slapping motion hitting her nose. Tapes, coins and old McDonald's cartons flew. As the car turned sideways, the wind was knocked from her lungs as the impact crushed her ribcage. There was a popping noise as ribs snapped. Her head whipped back into the headrest, the seatbelt tightened, digging in and causing deep friction burns to her neck. The wheels spun, churning up the snow and mud on the steep riverbank as the tyres attempted to grip, but they couldn't, and the car slid sideways into the river.

The car turned upside down in the water and rolled over as it sank to the bottom of the river. Nobody stopped to help, in the heavy snowfall perhaps nobody had even seen the car leave the road. Its wheels touched down gently on the bottom, causing a cloud of silt to rise. It wasn't too deep at the edge of the river; on a clear day, you might have been able to see the roof of the car a few meters below the surface. A huge bubble escaped from under the bonnet and rose steadily to the surface. There was a dull wrenching noise. The windscreen crack grew in size in short staccato motions. If you were watching as it grew, you might have thought it was happening in slow motion. But it wasn't, and nobody in the car was conscious to see it anyway.

'Mom, mom, come on! It's raining, let's go, come on let's go play in the puddles.'

Josh pulled on his wellington boots and dashed out of the house.

Josh took hold of her hand and led his mother out of the house and then ran away before spinning and kicking water at his mother.

The seal on the rear window gave way, spraying a thin jet of water onto Josh's face.

Laughing, she squatted down and flicked water onto his face.

'I'll get you back for that!'

Josh kicked water at his mother then laughed out loud as he jumped up and down in the water.

'Oh! It's going into my shoes, mom! No fair, my socks are getting wet!'

The footwell had filled up, and the water was nearly at the level of the seat.

Josh spun around in a circle looking for his mother, she wasn't there. She must be hiding.

'Mom, where are you?'

Water soaked through the fabric of the seat that Josh was sat on.

'Mom, I need the toilet, I really need to go!'

Josh looked down embarrassed as he saw the wetness spreading in his lap as he wet himself.

The water had now filled half of the car and was nearly at Josh's chin level.

'It's cold, feel cold mom!'

The water lapped at his chin. Josh's head tipped forward; his face now fully submerged in the water.

'Still cold, feel tired, very tired mom. Need sleep, sleep,

The cracked windscreen gave way, and dirty brown river water rushed in to fill the car.

CHAPTER TWENTY-EIGHT

Bankrupt Absolution

The frigid coldness of the water shocked her awake, but even so, it took her a moment to realise that she was still in the car and it was filling with water. It was at chest height now and rising steadily.

What the hell? I can't see, can't see — everything's blurred. What? How? Shit, shit, SHIT!

Then it came rushing back. The road, the car. Josh! She struggled to twist to see Josh, but she felt a grating sensation in her neck. Straining further, she felt her neck click, causing her to scream out in agony. She needed to be sick. Panic set in as the water suddenly covered her mouth, and she inhaled in a lungful of silty water.

It burns!

Coughing violently, she lifted her head to escape the rising water ignoring the intense pain in her neck and caught sight of herself in the rear-view mirror. The face that stared back at her was one of wide-eyed terror.

No, no, no!

Need to get out.

Or die.

She clawed at the seat belt release button. Her fingers crumpled like an empty glove when she tried to push the button down.

Not working?

Why is it not working?

Realising her hand was broken, she reached across to stab at the button with her other hand. It was hard to keep her face out of the water, so she angled her head up towards the roof of the car, desperate for any trapped air.

Out.

Or die.

Her clothes clung to her body, heavy, gripping. She found the seatbelt button.

Out

Pressed it. Nothing happened. Frantic now she repeatedly jabbed at it. Finally, she felt the tension release as it unclipped and floated up towards her face.

Die.

Or out.

She lifted herself out of her seat to press her face into the roof of the car, extending her life as she found an air pocket and sucked in air. It was the sweetest thing she had ever tasted.

Josh opened his eyes. Blood hung in the water near to his face. Swirling. Like his confusion. Then the panic came. Josh opened his mouth to shout his mother, but as he did so water rushed into his lungs. Josh banged on the window and gulped in another mouthful of the dirty river water. Then everything went black.

CHAPTER TWENTY-NINE

5

I know what you're thinking - but that wasn't me.

CHAPTER THIRTY

Obama don't care

Despite it only being late afternoon, the house was dark when they arrived back from the hospital. As Rachel slid the key into the lock, the door lurched open with a slight groan.

'Strange — are you positive you locked it,' asked Kim, 'maybe you forgot with all the stress you're under Rach? She added.

'No, the locks bust, it does this sometimes,' Rachel replied as she flicked on the lights.

'Are you sure?'

'Yeah, listen, Kim, thanks for coming with me, you know how much I hate that damn hospital,' Rachel said.

She hung her coat on top of another one in the hallway then went into the kitchen, to plug a charging cable into her phone, fiddling with it until the phone made a disinterested buzzing noise.

'It's no problem,' Kim replied, as she slid off her coat and tossed it onto the sofa. Rachel slumped down next to it and kicked off her shoes. Kim sat on the arm of the couch and looked at her.

'I don't know what to do anymore Kim. It's been months now and I've stalled as long as I can, but the hospital needs to see proof that the insurance documents exist or else they won't continue her treatment. Every search the hospital does, her name, her address, her past medical treatment, anything — it doesn't matter they all come up blank. All this and Josh is still missing. It's, I…'

Kim saw the worry etched into Rachel's face and she broke down, slowly at first; soundless sobbing and suddenly it came, loud and sad, causing her whole body to heave.

Come here Rach,' Kim said, sliding from the arm of the sofa, pulling her friend close and holding her tight. Kim closed her eyes as she felt the warmth of her friend's breath and the wetness of Rachel's tears on her neck. They felt hot and strangely arousing to her. Kim reluctantly broke the embrace and stared into her friend's eyes.

Even when you are upset, you are so beautiful, Kim thought.

She took hold of Rachel's hands; they were still cold from being outside. Rachel absently ran her fingers over the scar on the back of Kim's hand. Kim pulled her hands free and stood up.

'Come on let's have another look. We'll turn the house upside down. Leave no stone unturned. I promise you we'll find it this time Rachel.'

Rachel nodded and dried her eyes. 'Sorry, Kim, didn't mean to get upset.'

'It's all right — come on Rachel, let's get going,' said

Kim brightly, trying to cheer her up. 'What are we looking for anyway Rach?'

'I don't know, anything that looks official, I suppose,' replied Rachel, 'anything with medical numbers or maybe something like a prescription for some pills.'

'Shall we split up? Speed things up a bit?' Kim suggested.

'Okay, you look in the kitchen drawers. I've already looked, they're full of junk, but you never know. Oh, and can you feed Cujo for me please?' Rachel added as she headed upstairs.

'Sure Rach, no problem,' she replied, staring at the old dog slumped near to the dinner table. Kim went over and crouched down next to the dog who looked up at her and flicked out a single wag.

'I wonder what you think about me. Do you like me, Cujo?' She said stroking the top of his head and looking into his rheumy eyes.

'Fucking stinking animal, even when I'm here you have all of her attention, what do I have to do Cujo for her to see me?' she asked the dog. The long-haired German Shepherd just considered her dumbly.

'Do you? Do you like me?' She said, stroking his ears. Cujo tried to pull away wary at the tone in her voice, but Kim kept hold of his ears, increasing the pressure until he yelpcd in pain. Distressed, the dog wrenched its head away and stood up, baring his broken yellow teeth at her.

'I don't fucking think so,' Kim said, pulling the phone charger cable from the wall. She considered him for a moment then wrapped it around the dog's nose forcing his mouth shut and shoving him to the wall, pinning him there with her weight. The dog's eyes grew large with fear, and he struggled to escape, but Kim took hold of his throat and gripped tightly.

'Kim, come here I think I've found something!' Rachel called out excitedly as she rushed down the stairs.

'Who's a lucky boy then?' said Kim as she released her grip on the dog who, instead of running away or attacking her, just lay down submissively and trembled. Kim quickly unravelled the phone cable and threw it on the table, glancing at the dog as she walked back into the living room. He looked away when their eyes met.

Rachel held out the envelope to her friend and Kim gently took hold of her trembling hands.

'Look, Kim - I think this might be it'.

They sat down on the sofa and moved the empty cans and takeaway cartons on the table to one side then Rachel carefully laid out the contents of the envelope.

'So, Kim, look here,' said Rachel, pointing to the crumpled document, 'it says here that all medical costs will be provided for, up to... five hundred thousand!'

'Hang on, let me see,' said Kim snatching up the letter.

Rachel watched as Kim's eyes travelled along each line as she read the document, the frown on her brow deepening the longer she read. Kim gently set the document onto the table, smoothing out its creases and turned to look at Rachel.

'What?'

'Rachel, promise you won't freak out?'

'Okay - why?'

Kim shuffled closer to Rachel and pointed to

something on the document.

'Here, look.'

Rachel studied the line that Kim showed her. Hope crumbled into defeat in an instant.

'It expired two years ago.' Rachel said flatly, defeated. She was silent for what seemed like an age before she deliberately rose and screamed.

'That stupid bitch! More interested in getting wasted all the time instead of looking out for Josh and me!'

She rested her palms on the table and examined the words again then awkwardly picked up the table and hurled it against the wall, scattering cans and empty containers around the room. Kim grinned and looked on excitedly as the table hit the wall and knocked off the cover of a heating vent. Rachel stopped mid rage and stared at the hole in the wall.

'Rach, what's wrong?' Kim said.

'There's something inside it,' Rachel replied as she walked lethargically to the wall and knelt down.

'What is it?' Said Kim as she knelt next to her, thighs touching. When they peered inside, they saw a simple metal box, they turned to look at each other.

'What do you think is in it?' Kim asked.

Rachel shrugged her shoulders, 'only one way to find out,' she said, and then carefully removed the box from the hole and placed it down on the floor.

CHAPTER THIRTY-ONE

Blast from the past

They stayed sat on the floor with the box between them. Kim picked at a frayed corner of the rug as she looked at Rachel, who was staring vacantly at the box.

'Go on, Rach, open it.'

'What?' She replied, yanked out of her stupor.

Rachel stood up and paced around the room, running her fingers over the top of the sofa; Kim and Cujo tracked her with their eyes. Kim turned to look at the dog, and he held her gaze briefly before looking away. Rachel stopped and looked out at the street through the living room window just as a car passed by, seeming to slow before accelerating away.

'Who was that?' said Rachel, craning her neck to watch the car travel down the street.

'Who was who?' said Kim, moving to stand next to her and stare out of the window.

'Oh nothing, nobody, ignore me. I'm just feeling a little spooked, that's all. The house isn't the same without Josh here. You know he was noisy and messy, but I'd give anything to have him here with me right now.'

The red lights at the rear of the car became brighter as it braked to turn at the corner of the street. Rachel glanced up and down the road, the dull yellow light spilling out from a few of the houses opposite. A lamppost stuttered into life, casting its weak orange glow onto the pavement and the trees swayed in the breeze as a thin drizzle fell.

'Looks like it will rain — again, all it does is damn rain,' she said, dragging the heavy curtains closed, causing a little dust to fall as she did so.

Rachel picked up the metal box and shook it. It felt light, virtually empty, but not entirely, something rattled inside it. She rotated it to look at all surfaces for any markings, but the only thing she could see were light scratches from being put in and out of the wall.

'Feels empty Kim.'

'There must be something in it; otherwise, why would she hide it?'

'I guess so,' replied Rachel as she struggled to prise the lid off. She looked at Kim, 'we're assuming she put it in there, but it might have already been there before we moved here. The lids stuck, looks like it hasn't been opened in a while.'

Rachel gripped the box tightly between her knees as she dug her nails under the lid cursing to herself as she did so. Eventually, the lid snapped open, and the box fell to the floor, spilling its contents onto the threadbare rug. Kim picked up the letters and a coin that had fallen out and slumped back on the sofa.

Kim held the coin up and read its inscription: "Unity, Service, Recovery". The words were arranged in a triangle around a number one.

'What's that Kim?'

'Erm, looks like it's a one month alcoholics anonymous chip.'

Rachel shook her head, 'seriously?'

Rachel picked up a piece of paper and showed Kim the US Navy logo on the letterhead.

'What's that Rachel?'

'It's from the Navy to my dad - something about them wanting him to sign this letter to get some money for a finger injury. But he hasn't signed it.'

'Maybe he never saw it Rach.'

'Yeah, perhaps.'

'Rach, look — this one's addressed to your mom.' Kim said quickly changing the subject as she shuffled through the envelopes.

'And this one, and this one. None have been opened, and they are all addressed to her.'

Rachel sat staring at the envelope in her hands and spoke without looking up, 'all except this one — this one is for me.'

CHAPTER THIRTY-TWO
Empty Words

Rachel sat on the sofa and held the letter as if it was the most valuable thing in the world.

'Do you think it's from him — your dad?' asked Kim softly, squeezing Rachel's hands to stop them shaking. Rachel shrugged her shoulders and looked around. There was nothing in the room to remind her of him. No family pictures or cheap clutter that families collect. Things which meant something special to them once, but years later they can't remember what it was, yet they can't throw them away just in case. There were pictures of her and her mother and Josh in various combinations dotted around the place. Josh's paintings still clung to the fridge, kept in place by magnets which had lost their cheap plastic covers. Even faded and with curled corners, they were still reminders of Josh and his personality, yet it seemed as if her mother had deleted any reminders of her father.

Rachel looked carefully at the envelope; it was a different size and colour to the others, and it seemed to have become wet at some stage smudging the postmark, hiding its journey to her.

'Want me to do it?'

Rachel didn't respond.

'Rach?'

'What?'

'Want me to open it?'

'No, I got it,' she replied tonelessly.

Rachel looked down at the envelope and slowly tore it open. She took out its contents, a single sheet of white paper, unfolded it and placed it on the floor in front of them. Kim saw the expression on Rachel's face transform from one of optimism, into one of bewilderment or disappointment or something else, as she saw her eyes move across the words typed on the paper. Rachel shook her head and sat back on the sofa, closed her eyes and let out a deep sigh. Kim picked up the letter and read its single line aloud.

'37 13 40 N 43 26 14 E, what does this mean Rachel?'

'How the hell am I supposed to know,' she snapped back.

'All of this, the secret fucking box, the letters, this load of numbers, nothing makes sense, none of it.'

Kim waited a moment for Rachel to calm down.

'Wait a sec, these aren't just numbers Rach, there are two letters on there an "N" and an "E".'

'So? Still doesn't make sense. What is it? A code? Some secret offshore bank account I don't know about?' They sat in silence for a while before Kim spoke.

'Dunno Rach - shall I get your laptop so we can we Google it?'

Rachel nodded, 'Okay, you get it while I take Cujo out into the yard.'

Rachel watched as the dog circled and sniffed the ground, looking for a suitable spot before he squatted down to do his business. When he finished, he barked at something Rachel couldn't see and then followed her back into the house. Kim had already got the laptop started, and she watched her carefully type in the numbers and letters.

The first search responded with;

"Your search — 371340N432614E - did not match any documents."

'See Kim, I told you it was pointless.'
'Hold on Rach, let's try it with the exact spaces, same as on the letter' she said, fingers clicking on the keyboard as she adjusted the format of the search term. The result came back this time with a different response. It was a link to another web page.

https://tools.wmflabs.org/geohack/geohack.php?pagen ame=Kani_Masi&params=37_13_40_N_43_26_14_E_re gion:IQ_type:city

Kim clicked on the link, and a webpage opened, revealing a Google map image.
'Kani Masi - Where's that?'
'Well, it looks like it's in Iraq,' said Kim.

CHAPTER THIRTY-THREE

4

From the moment of conception, you are bound by body and blood. And although you are proud of everything they do, occasionally they do something that makes you want to scream out, "That's my girl!"

CHAPTER THIRTY-FOUR

Green Eyes Don't Suit You

Kim sat with her arms folded tightly across her chest, her jaw set tight.

'Listen, Kim, don't do your sulky little baby thing. I know you don't like him, but he is good with this computer stuff, maybe he can help,'

'Oh, I know exactly how you want him to help you,' Kim retorted, making speech marks in the air to emphasise the word "help".

Rachel stared at her.

'What's your problem? So, guys like me, deal with it. Perhaps if you weren't such a frigid bitch, you would…' A knock on the door stopped her mid-sentence.

'Erm, hello?' Steve said as he stepped into the house.

'The door sort of just came open,' he added nervously as he walked into the living room, aware that he had interrupted something.

'Hey Kim,' he said by way of a greeting, Kim nodded in response.

'So, I, erm — brought you some takeout, I figured you'd be hungry. Chinese - hope that's cool?' He said, looking around at the upturned table and cartons scattered on the floor. His eyes were drawn to the hole in the wall where the heating vent used to be.

'Sure, that's cool,' Rachel replied softly as she smiled at him, embarrassed at the messy room.

'I'll bring some plates, want some Kim?'

'Yeah, whatever you can spare for me, I'll have your left-overs if you like Steve?'

Steve found three clean forks and was about to say something but caught sight of Rachel looking at him. She frowned and shook her head, and he let it pass and followed her into the kitchen.

'Rachel what's wrong with Kim, she seems pissed that I'm here.'

'It's just been a long, long day that's all,' she replied, placing a hand on his shoulder as she looked into his eyes. He's got happy eyes she thought, even in the dim light of the kitchen the speckles of light green in his pupils stood out. When they went back into the living room, Kim had turned on the television and flicked through the channels before settling for a Jerry Springer rerun. They ate in silence as a scruffy mealy-mouthed woman called Claire was trotted out on stage before being grilled by Jerry on why she let her husband impregnate the teenage girl next door. A screen at the back of the stage displayed a scrawny looking girl holding a snotty nosed baby.

'So, to get this straight, you found a box with some old letters in it and one has map coordinates?' Steve asked.

'Yeah, someplace in Iraq,' Kim said, as she watched the track-suited teenager with bad skin walk on to the stage and sit opposite Claire.

'But that's as far as we got before we called you to help,' Rachel said, turning to Steve, 'thanks for coming over.' She felt her cheeks flush when he looked at her.

'It's okay, what do the other letters say?' He Asked over the noise of an on-screen argument which was being broken up by a bald stocky security guard in a tight black t-shirt.

'Turn the TV down, Kim. I don't know. Haven't opened them yet.' Rachel said.

'She daren't, they are addressed to her mom,' Kim added.

'I'm not scared Kim, I don't think it's right to open them. Maybe when mom wakes up, I'll ask her about them - I mean she must have a good reason to keep them unopened and then hide them in a box in the wall don't you think?'

A toothless lothario walked on stage with a strut, resplendent in his best tracksuit trousers and suede shoes to a barrage of heckling and insults from the students and other people who had no work to do sat in the audience.

'Okay, shall we get set up? I've brought my laptop; it's got a quad-core.' Steve said excitedly, not noticing Kim rolling her eyes and silently mimicking his words.

'Sure, what do you need?' Rachel asked.

'You know what he needs Rachel,' Kim paused before continuing, 'the map coordinates of course.'

Delighted that his audience had suitably chastised the husband, Jerry produced an envelope containing a set of DNA results.

Steve turned his laptop on and got to work, Rachel watched him, intrigued by the features of his face illuminated in the light of the computer screen.

'So, you're right, it is in Iraq.'

'Yeah, we knew that already,' Kim announced sarcastically, avoiding making eye contact with Rachel.

'Your father was a soldier, right? Did he serve in Iraq at all, the Gulf war in 1991?'

'No, well at least I don't think so. Mom never talks about him, and I remember when I found some photographs, she took them off me and burned them all. I only saved one, Steve.'

Talking about it sent her back years to when she was a young girl. Rachel remembered the men arriving in the middle of the night, their crisp, smart uniforms spoiled by their anxious faces. Rachel had tiptoed out onto the landing to listen but couldn't hear what they said. She recalled watching her mom; she had kept it together for her sake, Rachel guessed in case she woke her up and had to get her back to sleep. She held herself together but then the tall man who had done all the taking handed her a letter, and she broke down in tears. That was around the time she started drinking. Steve saw Rachel struggling to fight back her own tears, and he put a hand on her shoulder.

'Rachel, are you okay?'

She wiped her eyes and nodded for him to go on.

'What was he in, Army, Rangers?'

'No, Navy, I think. The picture I saved shows him wearing a blue uniform. Hang on I'll get it,' she said, standing up and striding towards the stairs giving Kim an expression that stated, "behave yourself".'

Steve continued tapping away on his laptop while Kim watched Jerry reveal that the baby did not belong to the man on the stage. The man looked gutted, and the two women just stared at each other bewildered.

Rachel handed the picture to Steve, who stood up to inspect it under the dim light hanging from the ceiling in the centre of the room.

'Looks like Navy. Do you recognise the insignia on his chest? What is it?'

Rachel shrugged her shoulders and leaned close to Steve, 'Dunno, I can't make it out. Can you?'

'No but we've got a high-resolution scanner in the computer science class. Perhaps if I scan it in, we can enlarge and enhance it. Can I take it with me?'

'Oh, leaving so soon, Steve? Something I said,' Kim muttered. They both ignored her.

'Steve, I'm not sure, it's the only one I've got.'

'I'll take good care of it. I promise,' Steve said, watching Rachel brush a stray hair from her face.

'Jesus, get a room will you before I throw up,' Kim said.

'It's alright, it's getting late, and I need to get back,' Steve, said, gently closing the lid of his laptop.

'Ring me as soon as you turn up anything, anything at all.'

'Will do, see you, Kim,' he said, as he walked to the door before turning back to look at Rachel.'

'Bye.'

'Oh, Steve, just before you go. What was supposed to be in the email you sent the other day?' She asked.

Puzzled, Steve shook his head,' I don't know your email address so I couldn't send you anything,' he paused as he opened the door, 'even if I wanted to.'

'Anyway bye,' he said as he closed the door behind him and left.

'Why don't you go as well Kim, I'm tired,' Rachel said as she stared at the mess on the floor and the hole in the wall that once hid the box.

'Bet you wouldn't be tired if he was still here, would you?'

'Oh, leave it, Kim. In fact, why don't you fucking leave, go on get out I'm tired of your bullshit tonight I don't know what's wrong with you.'

'Fuck you, Rachel!' Kim said as she strolled towards the door, and before she could respond, Rachel heard the door crash shut, leaving her all alone in the house.

Without realising she was doing it, Rachel began twisting and pinching the skin on her left arm, pulling on the skin and digging her nails in. She looked at her arm dispassionately and picked up a fork from the dinner table and dragged it back and forth over her left wrist, building up the pressure until the dull teeth of the fork broke her skin. She sat picking at the torn skin, the pain clearing her mind, and after a short while, she went upstairs and cried herself to sleep on Josh's bed.

CHAPTER THIRTY-FIVE

Boys in Blue

A noise outside dragged Rachel from her fitful sleep, and it took a moment for her to realise that it was the sound of a trash lorry, beeping and rattling its way down the street.

So, it's Friday then she thought, as she lay on the bed and looked around Josh's room, the pale morning light leaking in through the translucent Star Wars curtains. The room was as he had left it when he went out on that day, the day Rachel wished had never happened, the day he never came back. Books and toys remained scattered all over the floor where he played with them last: death-traps her mother called them after she'd stumbled on a toy car once. Rachel drew a deep breath and considered her arm, she couldn't see clearly in this light, but it was already yellow and purple where she had broken the skin. Josh's scent was still on the pillow and Rachel didn't want to wash it or the sheets to get rid of it. She looked up to the ceiling at the luminous stars and planets they had stuck on there together. Josh would waste hours lay on the bed with her, talking about the constellations and reciting facts about the planets, giggling when he said Uranus. Rachel's mind wandered as she listened to the clamour of the trash lorry fade into the distance. Once it had gone, the street was quiet, and she was drifting back to sleep when a loud knock on the front door startled her. Rachel sprung from the bed to peep through the curtains. She saw Steve on the porch, shifting his weight from foot to foot as he looked up and down the street.

Rachel knocked on the window and smiled at him, he looked up and smiled back at her, but it wasn't a happy one. She motioned for him to wait then dashed into the bathroom to splash water on her face and quickly drag a brush through her knotted hair. Rachel looked at herself in the mirror; she looked exhausted, dark circles were forming under her eyes, too much crying and too little sleep. A dull throbbing pain made her look at her wrist. It was sore, yellow and brown bruises had developed overnight. Embarrassment hit her like a train, and she couldn't make herself look in the mirror again. Rachel opened the door, and Steve came in carrying his laptop bag, she noticed that he was wearing the same clothes as last night.

'What no food this time, are you going off me, Steve?' She teased.

The state I'm in I wouldn't blame him though, she thought, pulling the sleeve of her top down to cover her wrist.

He hesitated, not knowing what to say to that, so he just came in and sat down.

'I found something,' he said, taking the laptop from its bag and pressing the power button.

Rachel sat close to him on the sofa, her thigh brushed against his causing him to tense momentarily, but he didn't move away. They watched the laptop go through its start-up routine for a moment; then he held up the photograph and pointed to her father.

'So, he was definitely in the Navy, the uniforms changed since then, but this is a Navy uniform,' he said excitedly.

'Okay, but we knew that already didn't we,' she replied.

'Yes, but that insignia on his shoulder got me thinking, I've seen Naval uniforms before, but couldn't remember them having that.'

He handed Rachel the photograph and she stared at the picture. She could just about make it out, but she could see now that all three men had the same insignia.

'So, I went into college, the security guard was an ass, but I told him I needed to get my USB stick I'd left behind in a computer and he let me in,' Steve said.

'Then I scanned your picture in and put it through an image enhancement program; it's so cool it cost a fortune and…'

The look that Rachel gave him cut him off before he could finish.

She sighed, 'come on, Steve, what does it show?'

'Okay, right, sorry. Look here at the insignia, it's grainy because it's an old picture, but look at the new one I made it's clearer on that one.'

'What am I looking at?'

Steve pointed at the picture, and Rachel noticed that he

had thin, delicate fingers, like a musician, a pianist perhaps.

'Look see the bird, that's an eagle, right?'

'Yes, I guess,' said Rachel, struggling to hide her irritation.

'And the anchor with the fork across it, look at it — do you see the fork? Well, it's not a fork, it's a trident actually.'

'Okay, trident, fork, whatever — I can see them Steve, but what is it I'm supposed to be seeing?'

Steve looked up at Rachel and ran his fingers through his hair before saying, 'Rachel that's the SEAL trident, you know the Sea, Air and Land SEALs?'

When she didn't reply he added, 'your father wasn't just in the Navy Rachel, he was a SEAL - he was a special forces soldier.' He paused before continuing, 'and I found something else.'

CHAPTER THIRTY-SIX

*Be careful **what** you wish for*

Rachel sat in silence, trying to come to terms with the fact that her father may have been a special forces soldier.

'Do you think that's why your mother doesn't talk about him, because she wasn't allowed to?' Steve asked.

Rachel stared at him, blankly. 'What do you mean Steve?'

'Well, I guess he wouldn't be allowed to tell her what missions he was on would he or even what country he had been to? Probably couldn't even if he wanted to.'

Rachel picked up the enhanced photograph and studied at it for a while. She looked at her father and examined his face, 'it's been so long now I wouldn't even recognise him if he walkcd right up to me in the street,' she said matter-of-factly.

She remembered the letter from the Navy about his finger and strained to look at his hands. Rachel could only see one, it looked like his little finger was shorter than it should have been, but she couldn't tell either way if it was or not.

Steve took hold of the photograph, 'Rachel, how did he die,' Steve asked gently.

She thought for a moment before speaking, 'well she never went into specifics, but she said something about him dying in a training accident when he was in Canada. His jeep crashed into a fuel tanker. It exploded killing him and everybody else in it - apparently the fire was so intense there was no way to identify any of the four people in the jeep afterwards.'

Rachel pinched her wrist through her sleeve, 'that's why we had a closed casket at the funeral — there was nothing to look at.'

Steve stared at Rachel's father on the photograph, almost willing him to confess his secrets.

'Didn't you think it was strange that he was working in Canada if he was in the Navy?' Steve asked as he watched her cover her wrist. There was a brown mark in the cuff where blood had seeped through.

'Yeah, well I quizzed her, but my mom wouldn't say anything about it, if anything she seemed embarrassed about it.'

'Embarrassed, how?'

'Oh, I don't know, I suppose that if he had to die, she would have wanted him to die a hero or something, not in an crappy accident. I looked on the Internet from time to time to see if there was anything about it in the news.'

'Was there?'

'Yes and no. There was something about an accident in Canada, but it didn't mention anything about a fire or anything. The only information I got was just about a driver who swerved from the road and drove into a lake and couldn't escape quickly enough.'

'Did he drown then?'

'Yeah but not in the water, it said that his fuel tank ruptured and filled his cab — he drowned in gasoline.'

'God, that's terrible Rachel.'

'I know right, when I asked mom why there was no mention of him, she became so angry and cried — a lot.'

'Perhaps he was there, if he was a SEAL, you know doing some training out there in the cold - maybe working with soldiers from another country?'

'Yeah but if that was the case, why didn't the Navy just confirm that they were training there then?'

'Don't know Rach. I don't know. Maybe they were operating a new type of weapon or super-secret technology they didn't want anybody to see.'

That's the first time he's called me Rach, she thought.

'You watch too many movies, Steve; I bet you think the moon landings were fake as well.'

Steve raised his eyebrows as he laughed, 'Well, now you mention it…'

Cujo barked twice as Rachel's cell phone rang and vibrated on the table; she picked it up and looked at it for a moment before she swiped across the screen to reject the call.

'Kim,' she announced, without being asked.

'I'll call her later once we're done. What else have you found? Don't tell me you found actual evidence that my father was this super-secret SEAL soldier?'

Despite trying to hide it, Steve heard the tiredness and strain in her voice.

'Not quite, at first, I used a VPN to access the TOR network on the dark web to see if there was any information about that place in Iraq.' He paused and looked at Rachel to see if she was following what he was saying - she wasn't.

'TOR network? Dark web?' She asked.

Steve thought about explaining, but instead he carried on speaking, 'Erm - never mind, so anyway there wasn't much out there about Kani Masi apart from a small entry on a bulletin board about it being the place that led to the Gulf war. You know the first one?'

'Why there, I don't understand, I thought it all took place in the desert?'

'Yeah, the war did, but Kani Masi was the place that one of Saddam's men, Chemical Ali they called him, tested a poisonous gas on some of their people which led to the assumption that Iraq had weapons of mass destruction. This dragged half of the world into the war and, if I was cynical, that and the fact they needed cheap oil of course.'

Rachel shrugged her shoulders.

'Sorry, Steve, I still don't get what you are trying to tell me. Poison gas, weapons of mass destruction, some dump of a village in the middle of nowhere; I'm struggling here, Steve - you said you had found something?'

She saw his jaw clench, 'listen, Rachel, you asked me for help, and I've been up all night...'

He got up to leave, Rachel took hold of his hand and pulled him back down to the sofa.

'Steve I'm sorry, you must think I'm an ungrateful bitch,' she squeezed his hand, 'come on, tell me what you've got.'

He nodded and continued, 'okay - so first of all the

dates of the alleged gas attack, I say allegedly because there is still controversy about if it ever took place, although a load of dead bodies would be pretty hard to deny. Sorry, I'm rambling here. It's the about the date of the attack and the date of the crash that killed your father,' he paused, 'they are the same.'

'Okay, so a coincidence then?' Rachel suggested.

'Yes, so I thought about that. It could be. But what if you needed to cover up somebody's death? Even if they are special forces, they would still need to have an official record of the death, wouldn't they?

He looked at Rachel, 'bear with me for a minute Rachel — I watched a movie about some soldiers who were taking part in a black ops mission somewhere they weren't supposed to be, South America, I think. Anyway, one of them got injured in an explosion or got shot or something and although the government denied that the mission had ever happened the injury showed up on his official record. So, I thought what better way of hiding somebody's death? What the SEALs do is classified so as long as the dates match, within a week or two I guess, they could get away with it. Somebody would have had to deal with the bodies, you know to bring the bodies back to the US, fill in the paperwork and stuff, so there must be a paper trail.'

Rachel rubbed her eyes, 'so did you manage to find it, the paper trail?' She asked, hopefully.

'No, but we know the crash in Canada happened around the same time as the gas attack in Kani Masi, that must mean something. I don't believe it's just a coincidence' Steve replied.

Rachel looked at the people in the photograph, wondering if any of them were still alive.

'I suppose with the war starting nobody would look too hard at the casualty reports, but if there's nothing about US soldiers being in Kani Masi I don't understand why the coordinates were in the box.' Rachel said.

They remained silent for a while as Rachel let Cujo into the yard and made them both a coffee. As she set the mugs down on the table, she looked at Steve for a moment before asking, 'the war was a combined effort, right? You know, lots of countries against Iraq?'

Steve nodded, unsure where she was going with this. Rachel took a sip of her coffee. Steve looked at her as she pressed her lips against the mug.

Her eyes grew wider over the top of it as she said, 'well, if lots of countries took part — maybe we're looking for evidence in the wrong place.'

CHAPTER THIRTY-SEVEN

3

You know it's always the wrong person who gets the credit. You can work for something all your life, and in the end, if you don't stand up for yourself, you get nothing, no recognition at all. Sure, I picked up a few trophies at school, but for all the things I had to do out there, I got nothing.

I hope they have positive role models in their lives now, someone to shepherd them in the right direction because there is nothing as important as bringing up children properly.

CHAPTER THIRTY-EIGHT

Safe Haven

'Okay, but where should we start, there must have been hundreds of countries involved in that war.' Steve asked.

'Well, Britain always follow America into any war without question. Why don't we start there?'

'Sounds like a plan,' Steve said, already searching the internet.

He said the words aloud as he typed away on the keyboard, 'Kani Masi, Britain, Gulf War.' Rachel watched him type; his nimble fingers dancing over the keys as he touch-typed. Browser windows opened and closed as he refined his search terms, quickly reading and rejecting information he didn't think was relevant. Rachel picked up her phone to call Kim and was just about to press her finger to the screen when Steve announced that he had discovered something.

'What is it, what have you got Steve?'

'Looks like you're right about the Brit's - they were in Kani Masi all right. Doing something called Operation Haven, but it sounds like it was some type of humanitarian mission, not a fighting one.' Steve said.

'But it proves they were there, doesn't it?' Rachel asked.

'Yeah but the dates don't match, they were there after the war had ended. Wait hang on let me read some of this. Operation Haven… Commanding Officer Hugo Tanner… in charge of providing safe zones for Kurds to come back to...' Steve said.

'No Americans, SEALs or anything?'

'Yes, Americans were there, but looks like only on a support basis, to provide food and equipment. Main people were British Marines from… Forty Commando and, wait, a civilian organisation called Doctors without Borders. I doubt there would be any secret missions going on with all those civilians around don't you think?' Steve said.

Rachel scratched at her wrist through her sleeve and Steve could hear the irritation in her voice when she spoke.

'So just more damn time wasted, the more we find out, the more questions we needed answers to. You know what Steve, I'm just about ready to forget about the whole thing, just go back to living my shit life, alone, here without Josh.' Tears welled in her eyes.
Steve sighed, unsure of what to do or say as he gazed at his laptop screen.

'Maybe you should go Steve, I need sleep.'

'Wait.'

She closed her eyes and swore quietly when she heard him begin typing again.

'Steve, come on I've just said…'

'Gotcha,' Steve said, practically bouncing up and down on the sofa.

Rachel groaned, 'what now, Steve?'

Steve looked at her and spoke hurriedly. 'Good old Wikipedia. Doctors without Borders page. I figured that if they had been in Iraq, they would have reported on it, you know for fundraising purposes or whatever, right?'

'Okay,' Rachel replied, stretching her sleeves down and holding them.

'So, this headline just stood out - "Medics nominated for Iraq award return to area." Return to Iraq Rachel - return, they had been there before! Listen to this… Dominic Fuller and Jim Dunn return to the area where they saved the life of an injured soldier.'

Rachel nodded slowly at Steve to carry on.

Steve paused. 'Okay - right, it goes on about those two working with the Marines again, them being recommended for an award, that sort of thing, that Officer, Hugo Tanner working with them to set up a hospital over there. And there's a quote from one of them, that Dominic Fuller guy…'

He stopped and stared at Rachel for a moment before looking back at the screen.

'So, he said, "it is a true honour to be part of Operation Haven in Iraq working with the Royal Marines. This visit will be extremely different because we have the language barrier to deal with now, at least the last time I treated someone out here they spoke the same language as us, albeit with an American accent."

Rachel stared at the letters addressed to her mother and the faded writing on the envelopes. I wonder if that's his writing, Rachel thought. She had never seen anything her father had written.

She traced her fingers over the words and without

looking up, said, 'thanks Steve, you've been amazing.'

'So, do you think your father was there, you know before this Operation Haven?'

'I don't know, I suppose it's possible. I know anyone can edit Wikipedia can't they, but the British were clearly there, there's no denying that is there? And these other men - the medics were there too, and I don't think they would make up being given an award, would they? They look like a pretty serious bunch, so I think they would make sure the page was accurate.'

Steve pulled on his lip, 'guess not, but the obvious question is, why would it mention saving an American at all if it was a classified mission?'

'Well, what is the date of the article?' Rachel asked.

'Early last year, so it's fairly recent, and maybe people were just not looking for anything referring to it. You know there's been the second Iraq war, Nine 11 and all the years that have been spent in Afghanistan, perhaps they've just been too busy.'

Rachel hesitated before saying, 'or there's nobody left alive to confirm or deny it. Right damn it - I'll take the letters with me to the hospital today and ask her about them, if she wakes up.'

'Cool, and I'll try to track down the guy in the article who got the award.'

'Great - call me if you find anything. Want to walk Cujo with me?'

Smiling, Steve said, 'can't, I need to get back home. Can I ask why, you know, why Cujo?'

Rachel sighed, 'well, like everything in my life, it's complicated. He was originally called Max, but after

Josh sneaked downstairs one night and caught the end of the Steven King film, he thought it was funny to call him that, and it just sort of stuck. Kind of suits him though doesn't it?'

Steve thought the dog looked more like a Max but agreed with Rachel anyway and they walked to the door together. Rachel opened it, and Steve moved to step through it, but before he could, she grabbed him, hugging him tightly.

'Thanks Steve,' she whispered as she broke off the embrace and kissed him on the cheek. She looked into his eyes for a long moment before saying, 'you'd better go - before we do something we might regret.'

CHAPTER THIRTY-NINE
Handgel

The hospital showed its age and looked even older in the flat grey light in that time just before the sun sets. The taxicab driver had babbled on about the weather, baseball and how badly the Red Sox were playing this year, but Rachel hadn't been listening.

When the taxicab pulled away, Rachel stood and stared at the tired building in front of her, the grimy windows seemed to absorb the fading daylight. In the centre of the building underneath the sign displaying the hospital's name, a flock of smokers had gathered wrapped up against the chill in an assortment of checked blankets. One smoker, a spidery Mexican looking man with bad skin, leaned in to say something to a stick-thin woman in a wheelchair and they both burst into fits of laughter, blue smog streaming from their mouths and noses. When they saw Rachel looking, they both grinned at her, the woman offering a toothless gap and the Mexican offering a tangled mess of rot and decay.

'Jesus Christ,' she thought, as she strode past them towards the sliding doors which opened with a gentle swish. Once inside, the hospital looked like any other; a clutter of confusing signage and pale yellow strip lights holding the carcasses of long-dead flies. A gaggle of receptionists sat behind their glass walls trying their best to look busy as they counted down the minutes until the end of their shift. There was a smell of disinfectant trying but failing, to hide the smell of vomit and bad drains. An obese black woman sat by the out-of-order vending machine, looked Rachel up and down and offered a sympathetic smile before going back to posting a status update on Facebook. On the right was a cramped shop selling overpriced sweets, trashy gossip magazines and almost dead flowers. Rachel went in to see if anything caught her eye that she could read to pass the time in this visit. She bought the latest novel by Steven King and a bag of gummy bears, paying the thousand-year-old woman behind the counter, telling her to put the change into the non-specific hospital charity collection box.

Rachel scanned the blurb on the back of the book as she walked back into the main lobby. Then she caught sight of him.

At first, she couldn't quite place him, but as he turned his head slightly to nod to the receptionist, she was certain it was him.

'Kyle? What are you doing here?' She said.

He continued walking, and Rachel didn't think he would stop, perhaps she was mistaken, and it wasn't him after all. But after a moment, he slowed and then turned to face her. Kyle stared at her, his eyes lingering too long on her breasts before he looked up and pointed at the hospital uniform he was wearing.

'Well obviously, I work here Rachel.' He responded condescendingly.

Rachel looked at his ill-fitting hospital uniform; probably worked here doing something low level she thought.

As if hearing her thoughts, he said, 'I've worked here since I graduated, heard about your mom's car wreck - really sorry, Rachel.'

'Thanks,' she replied, folding her arms over her chest; he still gave her the creeps.

'I've come to visit my mother. She's still not woken up, and they called to tell me they have transferred her to a different ward so a different doctor can care for her.'

'What's his name?'

'Who?'

'The new Doctor,' said Kyle.

'Oh. His name is Massey,' Rachel said, taking a scrap of notepaper out of her pocket and reading it aloud.

'Yes, Doctor Massey, Doctor Aiden Massey. Do you know him?'

'Yeah, he's not been in the hospital long though, he's probably treating your mom now. Want me to take you to him, it's no problem I'm going that way anyway,' Kyle said.

She nodded and they walked down the corridor, ignoring the uncomfortable silence between them. As they turned a corner, Rachel saw a girl being wheeled out of the hospital, her plaster covered leg sticking out in front of her, held in place by a splint. She was wearing a pair of loose-fitting shorts which had ridden up, and through the corner of her eye, Rachel saw Kyle stare at the girl's crotch as she came past. The girl didn't look

away from her phone screen, and Rachel saw Kyle smile
and nod to the orderly who was pushing the wheelchair.

'So, any news about your brother?' Kyle asked as he
fumbled with his ID badge. Rachel just shook her head,
reluctant to get into small talk with him and they walked
in silence for a few minutes until they came to an
elevator at the end of the walkway. Kyle stretched out
his ID badge on its retractable string and held it against
the black circular receiver next to the lift. Rachel
glanced at Kyle, who was looking at the numbers above
the elevator as it travelled down towards their floor. She
turned and was surprised to see the corridor behind her
was empty, apparently nobody needed to come this way
to visit anyone.

'Here we are Rachel,' Kyle said as the elevator door
opened. 'Just press number one and you want the second
door on the right once you get out.'

He lingered with his foot against the door in case it
closed.

'You not coming?' She asked.

'No, can't. I've got to help in theatre in half an hour.
Go on, you'll be fine.'

Rachel stepped into the elevator and turned to look at
Kyle as the door closed, he had stepped back to allow
the doors to close and smiled at her. Rachel forced
herself to smile back until the doors closed.

'Freak,' she said aloud to the scratched and dented dull
silver doors. The elevator juddered as it started its
descent to level one and she tapped her fingers against
the handles wishing she'd taken the stairs.

She hated being in confined spaces ever since her
mother had locked her inside a closet for two days when

she was six years old. Her mother had declared it was all her fault and that she shouldn't tell lies. She wouldn't believe Rachel when she said her mom's boyfriend at the time had come into her bedroom and put his hands under her sheets to touch her. Rachel remembered crying out, and he claimed he'd heard her shouting and had just gone in to check if she was okay.

'Just because you have a filthy disgusting mind,' her mother had said, 'not everybody else has you know!'

But after that he didn't come into her room again, and Rachel remembered how she'd struggled to screw a bolt to the inside of the closet door in case he did.

The tired ding of the elevator snapped her focus back to the present, and she stepped out into the corridor to visit the woman who had beaten her, let men touch her and continually argued with her.

The corridor was much the same as any other, perhaps darker as there were no windows to let in any natural light. Rachel stopped and looked around: same strip lights dangling from the ceiling, most of them working but to a few of them were struggling to light up. Old advice posters clung to the wall, some corners had curled over, leaving a cleaner area behind it. There were no signs she could see, and although she could detect the same disinfectant smell from before it was a little weaker and something made her feel grubby just being down here.

Halfway down the corridor, in front of her mother's room, a mop stood in a bucket of brown water. Looking down at the floor, Rachel was sure it hadn't been used recently. There were no chairs down here, outside of people's rooms, which she thought was odd as she set off towards her mother's room. Seconds before she arrived at it, a short man with light brown skin opened the door and strolled out, rubbing his palms together as if washing them. They were both startled. Apparently, he wasn't expecting her.

The man saw Rachel look at his hands, 'alcohol, disinfectant alcohol,' he announced, holding his hands up and wiggling his fingers at Rachel before he carried on dry washing.

The light above him flickered, and he peeked up at it over the top of his glasses.

He shrugged, 'Cutbacks. Can't afford it, you know, the people in charge, can't afford it. Pay themselves lots of money but have no money for lights.'

Rachel struggled to place his odd accent, definitely American but with a slight hint of something else.

He pushed his glasses back to the top of his nose and looked at Rachel, 'cutbacks, you know that's why she's down here. No insurance means she can't be on expensive ward, they are for people who can pay insurance.'

Rachel felt upset and stared at the strange doctor, despite his slight build and unassuming manner he unsettled her, and she was unsure what to say.

He pushed his glasses back up over his thin, slightly hooked nose, and then with his hands on his hips he nodded towards the door and said, 'you here for her?'

'Yes,' Rachel said, folding her arms across her chest, her wrist tingled demanding attention, but she fought the urge to claw at the skin, 'can I?'

The doctor rubbed his neatly trimmed beard then

nodded his head, 'okay, but not long, she not good today. Not long, okay?'

When he saw Rachel frown, he added with a thin smile that didn't quite curl at the edges, 'not long visit today I mean. She will not die today, I mean.'

Rachel let out a breath she didn't know she was holding, 'right,' she said, as she walked past the doctor who was squinting through his glasses at his pager.

Rachel saw him looking at her over the top of his glasses as she went into her mother's room. Although he didn't need to, he squirted alcohol gel into his hands from an almost empty wall dispenser and began dry-washing his hands again in a motion which reminded her of a fly cleaning its legs.

'Wow, she thought, 'he must really love the smell of hand gel.'

Rachel put her hand on the door and paused for a moment before she pushed it open and stepped into the room.

'Cutbacks indeed,' she said, looking around the room. It was dimly lit and sparsely furnished; just a bed, one of those tables on wheels and an uncomfortable-looking, oversized chair. The single strip light hummed and randomly flickered a warning that it would expire soon.

Rachel put the sweets and book onto the table, dragged the heavy chair up to the bed and sat down. When she looked at her mother, she noticed that they had removed the throat tube and in its place was a regular oxygen mask. Rachel stared at her face, when she wasn't scowling, she still had her looks, the crow's feet had come with age, but the lighting in the room accentuated her cheekbones giving her a harsh but attractive look.

I'll check the notes, this must mean she's getting better, Rachel said to herself as she stood and went to get the medical log from the end of the bed, but it wasn't there.

That's odd, maybe they didn't bring it down when they moved her.

There was no clock in the room, so she took out her phone to check the time but there was no phone signal down here.

Great.

Rachel took out the letters and laid them on the table in date order and looked at her mother lying in bed. Seeing her laid there, Rachel realised that her mother was helpless; depending on strangers to keep her safe, to keep her alive. When she had heard of the crash, Rachel had prayed; she remembered most of the words and added a part at the end about keeping Josh safe and taking her instead. What remaining faith she had in God had evaporated soon after when 'God' had saved her mother and taken Josh away instead.

For a while, it had been quite a high profile news story. A few news crews had parked outside her house looking for a quote from Rachel - she could hear them now, shouting to her as she walked down the street towards her home, "what happened to your Brother?" "How did your mother escape? Did she save herself and let your brother die?" It had captured the interest of the public who had little else to entertain them. What better than a story about an abusive mother who sacrificed her child to save herself. Rachel was convinced that the news interest had forced the hospital to take care of her mother despite having no insurance, but the reporters lost interest when there were no developments, and the hospital lost its patience shortly afterwards.

Rachel sat for a while, shifting in the seat, trying to find a comfortable position wondering how many people had sat there before her, waiting for someone to wake up - or not. She held up a letter and picked at the seal, causing it to tear and was just about to slide her finger inside the envelope when the door swung open, and the doctor walked in.

'Time.'

Rachel looked at him and shrugged her shoulders, 'what?'

'Time, it is time to go,' he said quietly. He looked at Rachel's mother, 'she tired, it is time for you to go.' He said matter-of-factly without meeting Rachel's stare.

'Okay Yoda keep your damn hair on!' She said gathering up the letters and standing, 'when can I come back?'

'Tomorrow is good, come tomorrow,' he said, ushering her towards the door.

Rachel hurried to the elevator which had been kept on this level by a fire extinguisher, preventing the doors from closing and anyone else using it. She entered the elevator, kicked the fire extinguisher out of the way and pressed the button to the upper floors. The doctor stood in the centre of the corridor watching her, and as the doors swished shut, he grinned showing a set of perfectly straight white teeth. The elevator juddered as it reached its destination, and when the doors opened, it surprised Rachel to see Kyle leaning against the wall waiting for her.

'C'mon I'll walk you out,' he said.

'Sure, whatever,'

'What's wrong Rachel?' Kyle asked as they walked towards the hospital's main exit.

'Don't you think he's a little odd, you know that doctor?'

'What do you mean?'

They made way for a porter pushing a bed toward an operating theatre, as it passed them, she saw it was the Mexican man she had seen earlier - he wasn't smiling anymore, if anything he had a desperate look about him.

'Thought you said you'd be in theatre?' Rachel said as the continued walking.

'What? Oh, that got cancelled, you know cutbacks, guess they can't get the staff or something.'

Rachel looked at him suspiciously, 'sure, cutbacks… that's what he said.'

As they approached them, the main doors to the hospital slid open, allowing a blast of cold air in and Kyle asked Rachel if she wanted a lift home.

'No thanks, think I'll walk for a while to clear my head. Nice seeing you again though,' she lied, turning to face him.

'Yeah you too,' he said reaching out to touch her arm. Rachel avoided his touch and walked out into the cold afternoon. Kyle watched her go before taking a deep breath and turning to walk back into the hospital.

CHAPTER FORTY

Sleep

'Who are you?' She pleaded with a weakness that embarrassed her, she felt pathetic, and she was not pathetic, she was strong.

He didn't respond and try as she might, she couldn't make out the features of his face, everything looked blurred, and when she looked at him directly, his features went fuzzy. She tried to look at him out of the corner of her eyes, but that didn't work either.

'Where am I?'

'What do you want?' She yelled, although she didn't think it was loud enough judging by the way he didn't react.

'Shhh,' she heard him say, and something convinced her he was rubbing his hands together in delight. The light in the room grew brighter, and it took her a moment to realise that someone had opened the door and come into the room.

'I said, where am I!'

She felt him take hold of her arm, his palm felt cold

and clammy; she struggled to move her arm but was too weak.

A man said, 'give it to me,' as his grip became tighter.

Her eyesight cleared a little and she saw the thick needle of the syringe he held above her. He brought it towards her arm, she tried to turn her head to follow its path but the intense pain in her neck stopped her from doing so. She felt a burning sensation as he inserted the point of the needle into a vein in the crook of her arm.

'Wha, wwhhhyyy ammm ere,' she slurred as the room spun and she tried to vomit, but before she could, she passed out, plunging into a deep coma-like sleep.

'Good stuff that Midazolam, nothing better to knock them out for 72 hours - well, nothing legal that is,' Kyle said to the doctor.

'Yes, indeed,' the doctor replied, looking at the woman in the bed. He took off his glasses, folding the arms together carefully before pointing at Kyle with them. 'Get rid of the needle. Leave no evidence.'

He slipped his glasses into a pocket, 'leave no evidence at all.' And with that, he walked out of the room, leaving Kyle alone with the woman.

Kyle pulled off the bedsheets, and after watching her for a while, he unbuttoned his trousers and climbed onto the bed.

'Don't mind if I call you Rachel, do you?' He said as he lay on top of her mother.

CHAPTER FORTY-ONE
The Letters

Kim was waiting on the porch, shifting her weight from foot to foot trying to stay warm, 'Jesus, Rach, you look freezing,' she said, as she saw Rachel approaching.

'Yeah, well, I've just had a very odd experience at the hospital, so I walked back to clear my head.'

'What do you mean?'

'You remember that freak Kyle, the spotty one, well he works there now,' Rachel said as she kicked her shoes against the door frame to clear the snow from them.

'Always wondered where he'd end up. Thought he'd get a job pumping gas or something, is he still the same old pervert he was at school?'

'Yep, he's still gross,' she shuddered, 'very gross, listen, Kim, I'm sorry about the other day, you now falling out because Steve was over,' Rachel said with a guarded smile.

'S'okay, Rach, forget about it,' Kim replied.

'I'm glad you got my text, thanks for coming over… I've decided to open the letters,' Rachel said as she fished her house key out of her pocket and inserted it into the keyhole. Before she could turn it, the force of the key sliding into the slot caused the door to swing slowly open. She shook her head and said, 'stupid door, you could have just pushed it open Kim and got a pot of coffee started.'

'Guess so,' she replied as she followed Rachel into her house, not bothering to clear the snow from her shoes.

'So did your mom say you could open them? Is she awake?'

Rachel turned up the central heating dial before sitting on the sofa, patting the space next to her for Kim to sit.

'No, she's still in a coma, they've taken that horrible down the throat thing away and put an ordinary oxygen mask over her mouth now, so that's good I guess, but the ward she is on now is an absolute dump Kim, and I think she's the only one on it. And her Doctor is a creepy little man.'

'Creepy how?' Kim asked.

'Dunno, he's foreign, not being racist, but I'd preferred her to have a real America Doctor, oh and he repeats himself like some sort of real-life Yoda. Anyway, forget about him, shall we do this?'

Rachel held up the oldest letter. Kim nodded, and Rachel carefully slipped her finger under the seal, tearing the envelope until it opened. She lifted the letter out, unfolded it and held the pale white paper out in front of her.

'What does it say Rach?'

'Normal stuff at the top, his service number 498 etcetera, that sort of thing. Okay listen, I'll read it.'

"To my dear loving wife,

I hope that this letter finds you safely and Rachel is behaving herself, well as best she can! We are not up to anything interesting - again! I'm sure that they send us to these places just to test our patience, you know I love my team, but when you spend a long time with them, it can become a little grating. All their little habits and odd smells! So, I spend most of the time reading those old Stephen King books that you made me bring or playing on an old Sega, getting quite good as well if I say so myself. I'm thinking of getting one for Rachel, what do you think? We're just on a few rest days out of the jungle at the moment to dry out, it's always raining here, and although the canopy is quite thick, it still gets through. I'm sick of it, when we aren't wading through streams or crossing rivers, we are ankle-deep in dirty muddy puddles. Come to think of it Rachel would like it - jumping in all these muddy puddles, is it still her favourite? Can't wait to splash in them with her when I get back.

I know you like warm places, but you wouldn't like it out here, it's hard to breathe, there's hardly any wind and the humidity is really thick, as soon as you move you are covered in sweat. I've lost count of the number of times that I have been bitten by mosquitoes, the damned things are everywhere, always buzzing around my ears. I swear that if I never hear their high pitched whine again, it will be too soon. The insect repellent they give us melts plastic but won't keep them away! Anyway, I need to go now, so give Rachel a huge squeeze from me and tell her I love her, and I'll see her soon. Please write back soon,

Your ever-loving Husband

Rachel passed the letter to Kim who reread it slowly.

'Well, that was a bit of an anti-climax.'

'You can say that again, Kim.' Rachel said, taking the letter back from Kim and searching for hidden meaning in the words, but finding none. 'I'd have thought he'd have more to say to her?'

'Dunno Rach, guess if he was stuck in the middle of the jungle or wherever he wouldn't have had much time; it must be hard writing with a load of guys around you.'

'Maybe, Steve's coming over soon - he's found out a lot of information about some covered up operation in Iraq. Oh, and it turns out that my dad was a special forces soldier who died in a training accident in Canada, only that he didn't as he wasn't there because he may have been in Iraq at the same time!' Rachel blurted out.

'God, Rachel slow down! What do you mean, special forces?'

Rachel exhaled slowly, 'yeah apparently he was a SEAL, Steve took his picture in and scanned it, look, see that insignia?' Rachel said, handing Kim the enlarged photograph.

'Do you see?'

'Yes, I see it - are you sure that means he was a SEAL?'

'We looked it up, and that's definitely the insignia, the current version is a bit different, but yes.'

Kim studied the photograph, 'so who are the others? They look like an odd bunch, all different sizes but I mean just look at how big that black man is. Surely someone would recognise him?'

'No idea Kim, I guess they are his teammates, but I can't be sure.'

They sat in silence for a while, Kim picked up the letter and read it again and Rachel stared at the two other letters, subconsciously picking at her wrist through her sleeve.

She pinched herself hard and suddenly said, 'Kim I can't wait for my mother to wake up, I'm going to open the other letters.

"To my dear loving wife,

You do love me, still don't you? I suppose you have just been too busy to write back to me or the letters haven't arrived yet? So anyhow things are pretty much the same here, same shit different day, you know how that is, don't you? Usual stuff for us out here, work, eat, sleep repeat, it's tiring, but it beats working in an office I guess. We're doing really difficult jungle navigation, it sounds odd, but you can't tell if you are actually going up or downhill because the fauna is so thick. The other day I leaned against a tree without checking and got bitten by a load of big red soldier ants that got into my jacket. None of my team warned me, they just watched them walk down the trunk and into my clothes - I would have given them a dressing down that they wouldn't forget if we weren't fully tactical. It's tough you know, being on a hard routine, not being able to cook your rations in case the smell gives your position away. Anyhow Kama is a bitch, a little while later Rocky got his foot stuck in a mangrove root and nearly broke his leg when he fell over - that'll teach the big black bastard a lesson won't it?

We set up an observation post next to a pool this morning before we came in and there was a load of those little skating insects dancing around each other in circles on the surface. It reminded me of last Christmas when I was on leave, and we took Rachel to Boston Common, and we ice-skated on the Frog Pond. Do you remember, you were pathetic and could hardly stand up? As usual, I had to teach Rachel how to do it, I sometimes wonder what you actually do with her when I'm not there. Do you remember how cold it was? I swear it was minus ten, but she still wanted a hoodsie, didn't she? I think that once she got used to the heat Rachel would like it out here, there's lots of biting annoying insects, but there's also lots of really nice things. You know how she loves butterflies; well they are so big out here. It's a wonder that they can actually fly, they can obviously, but they look so awkward lurching around. The spiders are big too! I still hate them - don't you dare tell anyone, especially Rachel. Anyway, I need to go now to get ready to go back out on patrol so give Rachel a big hug from me and write back soon.

Your loving husband.

Kim listened as Rachel read the letter to her again then asked, 'do you think this Rocky he talks about is the big black man in the photo?'

They heard a car pull up and shortly afterwards there was a soft knock on the door. Rachel went to answer it; as she walked, she said, 'I don't know, it could be, but the thing that bothers me is the tone in the letter. Do you know what I mean?' She opened the door and let Steve in, and they hugged briefly before he sat down in the chair opposite Kim.

Steve smiled at her and Kim forced herself to smile back at him before saying, 'what do you mean, a different tone?'

Rachel sat on the arm of the chair next to Steve before saying, 'Oh, I don't know, it's just that there's swearing and I do remember going skating, but it was my mother who taught me how to do it. And I think they argued, and he wouldn't buy me an ice-cream in case I got fat, and nobody would want me when I got older.'

'Why would he make something like that up?' Steve asked quietly.

'My mom always said he was a liar, maybe that's why he wrote that.'

'Rachel says you found out a lot of useful stuff last time you were here, did you find anything else out Steve?'

Steve looked at Kim and then at Rachel; he seemed concerned about something. He shifted the laptop bag onto his knees, 'I found something, but perhaps you should open the final letter first - things might make more sense that way?'

Rachel shrugged her shoulders and roughly tore the envelope open, 'okay here goes, listen carefully I'll read it all. It starts with our address then his name and service number, 498-45-6 etcetera.'

"Dear wife,

You better have a damn good reason why you have not written to me, it's been three weeks, and I have not heard anything from you. Even if you don't want to speak to me, why are you being such a bitch and not at least telling me how Rachel is doing? Everybody else out here is getting letters so I know there's no problem with them being shipped over here to us. I swear to God if something has happened to my little girl and you are hiding it from me, I'll fucking kill you. Do you hear me? I mean it, she is the only thing good in this world for me, I think about her every day. I hope that you gave her the necklace that I left, you better have because you know she doesn't lie to me. She might do to you, but not to me, I don't care if you claim not to be religious, but I am, and she wanted to it. Even if you write to me now, I probably won't get it for a while as we are moving from here now, I can't tell you where but let's put it this way, I'll have the best damn tan in the neighbourhood when I come home once it's all over. Make Rachel write to me, I don't care if you won't, but please make her write to me - you fucking better!

Your husband.

'Whoa okay,' Kim said slowly, 'that wasn't nice.'

'No, it wasn't, makes me feel bad. Perhaps that's why mom's been such a bitch all this time - he made her that way.' She turned to Steve, 'please give me some good news, Steve.'

He looked at her and saw that she was welling up on the verge of crying. As he opened his bag to take his laptop out, he noticed a small brown patch of blood on her sleeve. His gaze lingered there a little too long, Rachel saw where he was looking and covered it with her other hand.

'Can't give you anything good, Rachel, everywhere I look turns out to be a dead end.'

'Okay, Steve let's have it then, what have you found?' Rachel asked.

The slight whir of the laptops fan was all they heard as they waited for Steve to begin.

'Right, so I looked into the Brit soldiers first. Operation Haven definitely happened, it's on their Ministry of Defence website; so that's a fact. I did the normal searching things for the soldiers and I got a name, Ivan Hawley. He was in charge of some marines and some doctors - you know the Doctors without Borders ones?' He asked.

Rachel nodded and looked at Kim, 'they were there to set up safe areas, but they also seem to have been based at Kani Masi.'

Kim frowned and urged Steve to continue.

'Great, so can we contact him then?' Kim asked.

'Afraid not, the reason I found his name was because it came up as an obituary in a newspaper. Three years after Operation Haven - a year before he could retire, someone killed him in a shoot-out at a vehicle checkpoint in Kosovo. The poor man pulled over a car full of local gangster types who shot him and then drove over his body.'

'And let me guess — you couldn't find any information about the marines he was in charge of in Iraq?' Rachel said, fighting the urge to pull up her sleeve and drive her nails deep into her flesh.

Steve paused, 'you got it, a dead end there. So, then I did searches for the doctors who worked with him — and this is where things get a little weird, well — a little weirder.'

Kim said, 'hang on. So, let me get this right. The British were in Iraq, at the place we found in the envelope?'

They both nodded to her. She continued, 'the only

person you could find to verify that Americans were there as well, was killed in Kosovo?' Kim looked at Steve, 'so what could be weirder than that?'

He took a deep breath and continued, 'so I found the hospital they said the doctors were from and phoned them, I got passed around a while until somebody would help me. I told them I was a relative planning a special birthday present for Dominic Fuller. They found information about the two doctors; Jim Dunn and Dominic Fuller but their records showed that they had only been working in Turkey around that time. So I said that couldn't be right because on Wikipedia it said they were in Iraq and you know Wikipedia never lies, does it?' He smiled at the two girls - they didn't smile back.

He shifted in his seat.

'Right, okay, so I told her she was wrong and to look it up herself, and she did.' He paused, 'there was nothing there.'

Puzzled, Kim asked, 'what do you mean there was nothing there, I thought you said you'd seen it?'

'I did - before I phoned them there was stuff about the medics on there - I swear, so I checked on my laptop while I was speaking to her and she was right, but I had a copy in my web history so I know it was there once.'

Rachel felt her wrist itch, 'so online it's gone? All of it?'

'Yes, no, well not quite I mean,'

'Jesus, Steve, what is it, gone, not gone, what!' Rachel said, her wrist was craving attention now, begging for her touch.

Steve frowned, 'okay, well the entry was still there, it had just been changed, the entry about the award was gone, and someone replaced any mention of Iraq with Turkey. And I can't find any mention of the two medics anywhere else on the Internet, nowhere on Facebook or anywhere on social media.'

'Great, another dead end, in fact, not just a dead end it's a damn stonewall,' Rachel said, clenching her fists, feeling her nails dig into her palms.

She grabbed her cell phone and dialled the hospital, pacing around the room as she waited to be connected.

'C'mon, c'mon. God, how long does it take for you to fu... hello, hello yes, I want to speak to somebody about my mother. What? Yes, I'll hold.'

She heard a different voice this time over the crackling connection.

'Yes, I want to speak to the doctor who is looking after my mother, Mrs Rogers.' Rachel went silent and looked open-mouthed at Steve and Kim.

'Can you say that again? She's checked herself out. That's ridiculous, I saw her today, and she was still in a coma - the doctor said she was getting better but there's no way she's well enough to leave.'

Rachel listened to the impassive voice and then said, 'What are you talking about? Which doctor? The small one - Massey, that's it, Doctor Massey,' The line went dead for a second and Rachel thought they had hung up when she mentioned his name. It seemed like an age before the voice returned.

'What do you mean nobody by that name works there, I saw him, I went down to the other ward to see him, I....'

The voice at the other end of the line cut her off

abruptly.

'What the hell do you think I mean; I went down in the elevator to see him on the ward.'

Kim watched Rachel listen to the voice again and saw her shake, she stood up and held onto her shoulders,

'Rachel, what's wrong, what have they said?'

Rachel looked at Kim, blinking rapidly as she said,

'they said the ward isn't actually a ward; it's a storage area which hasn't been used for years.'

She shook her head, 'and there's no one called Doctor Massey - never has been!'

And with that, she stood there as if frozen to the spot.

Kim looked over at Steve who was already stuffing his laptop into his bag and pulling out his car keys.

'Come on Kim, let's get her into my car and get over there, find out what the hell's going on.'

CHAPTER FORTY-TWO

Visiting Time is Over

Steve pulled up outside the hospital, and they rushed inside, ignoring the shouts of the receptionist telling him he couldn't leave his car there. As if on autopilot Rachel ran directly through the corridors to the elevator and pushed the button repeatedly until she heard it groan into life as it travelled up to them. The doors swished open and lazily slid shut as if the elevator was deliberately trying to slow them down. The elevator seemed to take an age, juddering all the way to the ground floor, the light overhead flickered. The doors clattered open to reveal the long dark corridor as they stepped nervously out of its metal carcass. The corridor was the same as Rachel recalled, even down to the flickering lights and mop bucket in exactly the same place.

'Come on, she's in here,' Rachel said, as she ran towards her mother's room.

She swung the door open and quickly went into the room, followed immediately by Kim and Steve.

'Jesus, Rachel, what is this place,' Kim said, as she took in the scene in front of her, which amounted to not much more than a bed with a chair next to it.

Rachel was shaking her mother, she felt so thin, like a bag of bones. Without turning around, she yelled at Steve to look for a wheelchair.

'On it! I'll carry her out of here if I need to Rach,' he said, as he hurried out of the room.

'How long were they going to keep her down here for?' Kim asked.

Rachel didn't reply, 'Mom, mom wake up - can you hear me, wake up - come on damn it!'

Kim moved to the other side of the bed and was about to sit down when Steve barged through the door, pushing a wheelchair in front of him.

'Any change?' He asked. Rachel seemed to have not understood him and Kim's shake of her head answered his question.

'I've found these,' he said, holding up a handful of syringes, 'perhaps these will wake her up?'

Rachel turned and stared at Steve, 'are you fucking insane? We're not sticking them into her, who knows what they will do to her?'

'Actually, I do,' said Kyle as he stepped into the room.

He wasn't wearing his hospital uniform now; he was wearing light blue jeans, a scruffy sweatshirt and his lank, greasy hair seemed plastered to his skull. He smoothed his fringe out of the way, wiping his hand on his jeans and even in the weak light of the room they could see the patchwork of blackheads and pimples peppering his face. Kyle walked past Steve and stood at the end of the bed. He stuck his hands in his pockets and

considered first Rachel and then Kim, meeting her eyes
before he looked her up and down, smirking when he
saw her shift uncomfortably. Rachel stood up and
gripped hold of the cold metal bed frame, picking at its
flaking paint, frowning as the sharp edges cut into her
fingertips.

Rachels tone was flat, 'what are you doing down here,
Kyle, have you got something to do with keeping her
down here like this?'

He shrugged his scrawny shoulders, 'cutbacks I
guess,' he said absently.

Rachel launched herself at him grabbing him around
the neck, the force of her attack catching him off guard,
pinning his slim frame against the wall. He didn't even
have a chance to take his hands out of his pockets. He
didn't resist, if anything he seemed to be pressing his
body against her. When Rachel realised what he was
doing she dragged him away from the wall and twisted
around. She let go of his neck, but the motion made him
tumble backwards over the wheelchair and crash to the
floor. Despite being winded, he looked up at Rachel and
laughed.

'Are you for real asshole,' Steve said, starting towards
him. Rachel reached out a hand to block him; she
seemed calm, but Steve saw an intense rage in her eyes
stopping him dead in his tracks. Kyle didn't get up, he
lay on the filthy floor, his head still but his eyes flashed
swiftly between the three of them before looking at the
needles in Steve's hand.

Rachel pointed at the syringes, 'does she need these?
Is this what's keeping her alive - how many does she
need, one… two?' She said, struggling to keep her tone

even, but they all heard her voice breaking.

'Give them to me!' she demanded, 'you two hold him down - we'll see if he's still smiling when I stick this into his neck,' she said.

Steve passed them to her, his hands were shaking. Rachel flicked the plastic safety cap from a syringe with her thumb. Kim and Steve looked at each other as they knelt down and held his arms tightly while Rachel held the needle close to his face.

'Tell me what these do, Kyle,' Rachel said, as she moved it closer to his face. His eyes grew wider, and then he went cross-eyed as he tried to focus on the long thick point being held over him.

Kyle grimaced, showing food trapped in the gaps of his teeth, 'don't know nothing,' he spat back at her.

'What are you doing down here then, did you follow us? Where is that asshole of a doctor?'

Kyle raised his eyebrows, 'dunno what you're talking about.'

'No?' Rachel said.

'Get off me you stupid slut or you will...'

'No,' Rachel said, as she stabbed him in the neck with the syringe. Her thumb hovered over the plunger, ready to force the contents of the syringe into his body. Kyle winced but tried to remain as still as possible, beads of sweat appeared instantly on his forehead, and he broke wind.

Rachel wiggled the needle from side to side, 'still not talking you disgusting prick? I swear I'll inject you with every needle I can find in this hospital, you'll end up looking like a fucking pin cushion!'

Kim shifted, 'Rachel come on - let the police deal with

this.'

Rachel looked at her, 'shut up Kim, don't turn into a damn pussy on me now!'

'I'm not, but you might end up killing him if you inject that into him!'

'Won't,' Kyle whispered from beneath them and they all turned to look at him. He was speaking quietly, trying not to move, they could see his jaw muscles clenching inside his pock-marked cheeks.

'I mean, it will... if too much... more than one at a time will cause an overdose... one knocks you out for a few days...' he rambled on.

Rachel looked down at him and started to say something then stopped and looked at her mother lying in the bed, 'so she's okay?' She asked.

'Kyle nodded carefully and then whispered, 'nothing wrong with her.'

'What do you mean - so she's just drugged to keep her asleep?'

He nodded again.

'But why - why would you do that, Kyle, what the fuck?'

'Him, he made me do it,' he stated flatly.

'Who Kyle, who made you do it,' Rachel leaned closer to his face.

'The doctor made me forge the documents to show her being discharged. Then he made me move her down here, there's nothing wrong with her, he kept injecting her to keep her asleep - I don't know why, but he just kept doing it, every few days. I didn't want to do it, Rachel, he forced me,' his cheeks glowed red, 'to keep her clean - you know wash her and stuff.'

The thought of him touching her mother repulsed Rachel. Her hand shook, causing him to cry out in pain as the needle tore at his skin as she shifted away to avoid his sour breath.

She turned her head to look at him again, 'hang on, Doctor Massey? Do you mean him? When I phoned, they claimed he's never worked here – they'd never heard of him. How'd it possible that he worked here, but they never saw him?'

Kyle's hair was plastered to his head with sweat and spittle had formed at the corners of his lips, he gasped, 'when we brought her down here he handed in his notice and quit - we'd come in through the morgue when we knew people weren't working or had left for their lunch breaks. Anyway, he still had his ID badge and none of the lab techs down there would question why a doctor would be there. He spent most of his time down here anyway, people probably never saw him, and as far as the people upstairs were concerned, he'd disappeared.'

'Where has he gone?'

'I don't know - he was due to come here this later, he told me to meet him here. He mentioned something about needing to teach you what it was like to lose someone you loved.'

Rachel frowned, unsure what he meant by the comment.

'Call the police Rachel - this is kidnapping, maybe even attempted murder. God knows what else they've been up to down here.'

Rachel asked, 'is it true she will wake up if she stops being injected?'

Kyle nodded.

'Then I've got an idea,' she announced, pulling the needle from his neck and holding it so close to Kyle's eye that his eyelashes brushed against it when he blinked. Tears formed in his eyes.

'You're going to take the tubes out of her arm and get her ready to move,' she paused, enjoying the power she had over him, 'blink twice if you understand.'

He did.

'We're taking her home… then you are going to take us to him.'

CHAPTER FORTY-THREE

*Be careful **who** you wish for*

Steve accelerated off the slip road to join the traffic on the northbound highway and glanced at Rachel in the rear-view mirror.

'You sure Kim will be okay with your mom, I mean won't she be confused when she wakes up at home on the sofa and you're not there?'

'Yeah she'll be fine, anyway, this prick said they injected her again this morning, so she'll be out for a while — maybe 'til tomorrow. Honestly, I can't wait for this nightmare to be over.'

Kyle was sat in the passenger seat, his hands bound tightly together with packaging tape. He was sat upright, his head pressing tight against the headrest, secured in place with one of Josh's scarfs.

Rachel hated the idea of something that had touched Josh's neck, touching him, but time was against them once they had settled her mother onto the sofa and they were rushing to the doctor's house in case he returned to the hospital and realised they were gone.

Kyle couldn't remember the exact address of the

doctor's house, but he'd been there once before to carry in some heavy medical equipment for him. With Rachel pressing the tip of a kitchen knife into the base of his skull he managed to provide a reasonable description of what the street looked like, nevertheless.

Steve had located the general area using Google Maps, and then by using its street view function, Kyle guided him to a location to the north of the city near to Dogtown Common.

They travelled in silence for a while, the stress and the motion of the car was making Rachel drowsy, but she fought to stay awake. The kitchen knife was a reassuring weight in her hand, and she could feel the syringes in her trouser pocket pressing into her leg. There were seven of them; enough, Kyle had said to keep somebody asleep for weeks if they timed the doses correctly.

The thought of somebody purposefully drugging her mother made her feel sick, and she gave Kyle a sharp prod with the knife, drawing a red pinprick of blood. After a while, they swung off the freeway onto a minor road and followed its twists and turns until they saw the sign for Dogtown Common. Steve pressed the brakes to slow down as they crossed over a narrow wooden bridge which creaked under the weight of the car.

'Not long now,' Steve said, glancing at the map on his phone that he had wedged in the dashboard, 'bout half a mile.'

Rachel saw his eyes in the rear-view mirror and nodded at him. They crested a hill before following the winding road, descending towards the houses at the bottom of the u-shaped valley.

The houses had been built for immigrant workers to house them while they worked on the 'Big Dig' construction project to build road tunnels under the city of Boston, but they were now all unoccupied and dilapidated. Rachel recalled reading something about the government buying all the houses as they needed to build a new reservoir to provide water to the continually expanding city of Boston. Its location in a vast natural depression made it the ideal place to be flooded and developed. The people had moved out, but the government were dealing with some kind of financial crisis and had shelved the project. The area had stood empty for years; a once-thriving town now forgotten and waiting to be drowned.

Steve stopped the car at the side of the street and pointed to a house at the end of a short driveway.

'That it?' He said, gesturing to Kyle, who didn't answer until Rachel pressed the tip of the knife into his neck.

He strained to nod.

Rachel hit the back of the headrest hard with the palm of her hand, 'are you sure?'

'Yes, yes, I remember that spindly little tree out front. Do you see it?' He croaked.

Rachel ignored him as she looked at the house until Steve eventually spoke, 'what shall we do, Rachel?'

'Looks empty - no cars there, just drive up and we'll just knock on the damn door to see if he wants his creepy little friend back.'

Apprehensively, Steve put the car into gear and drove onto the driveway of the house, the car's tyres making crunching noises as they rode over dirty gravel and broken glass. It was a small single-story house, set back and sideways on to the street. It was built in the colonial style with large sheets of overlapping wood, once painted bright-white, but some time ago somebody had sprayed graffiti over the walls and windows. Every streetlight was either smashed or not working. Daylight was fading, and despite the poor light, the general state of disrepair and rot was clear to see. The whole area looked filthy, lots of windows were smashed, and flaking paint on the door fluttered in the faint breeze. Rachel untied the scarf then got out of the car easing the door shut carefully.

Without looking away from the house, she opened the passenger door and waved the knife in front of Kyle.

'Out,' was all she said, turning to watch him struggle to get out.

The house had a squat brick built chimney attached to one side of it, and Rachel studied it carefully for a moment, checking to see if any smoke rose from it. Satisfied that there was not, she pushed Kyle towards the front door.

'Try the handle,' she ordered him, and Kyle took hold of the round brass knob which rattled as he turned it with his bound hands. It was locked.

She prodded him in the bottom of his spine with the tip of the knife, 'kick it in,' she told him impassively and stood back as he kicked at the door, almost bouncing off of it. Realising it wasn't working, suddenly filled with male bravado, Steve pushed Kyle out of the way and slammed his shoulder against the door. It burst open, taking pieces of the crumbling door frame with it. The force of the impact carried Steve forward a few meters into the house, and he stumbled in the dark corridor before quickly stepping back out, dusting his shoulder off and looking around nervously.

They made Kyle go in first, Rachel found the light switch behind the door and switched it on illuminating the hallway. The walls were covered with wood chip wallpaper which was peeling away from the wall and the smelt of damp was overpowering. The floors were bare except for a dusty mat just inside the door which said, "Welcome Home" on it. In line with the front door was a small kitchen area and a quick search revealed that it contained only a kettle, a few mugs and a tea strainer. Off to the right, was a small square room with a sleeping bag on a dirty mattress. To the left was a room about the same size, but this one had a desk with a battered wooden chair underneath.

On top of the desk was a television hooked up to a VHS video recorder. Looking utterly out of place at the back of the room was a hospital bed complete with a full saline drip hanging from a wheeled stand. Steve pushed Kyle into the room, and he fell against the table, his hands grabbing at the surface to stay balanced, he gripped the edge of the table tightly to steady himself.

When her eyes had adjusted to the light, Rachel looked at the shelf above the desk, which had an assortment of videotapes with people's names on them. Rachel motioned for Kyle to sit on the floor in the corner and pressed the switch on the wall turning on the television and video recorder.

As soon as it turned on, the video recorder spat out a tape with the name Charlotte written neatly on it. Rachel pushed it back in and slumped down in the chair, Steve stood off to the side of her, in front of Kyle, and when she glanced at him, Kyle looked down at the floor.

The video started off fuzzy, with vertical lines running across the screen until it cleared. There was no sound, and it took Rachel a moment to realise what she was watching. The screen showed a hospital bed in a room like the one they had kept her mother in; there was only a bed and a chair in there. Rachel watched for a while before pressing the fast-forward button until she saw movement, then stopped it to see what it showed.

A young girl was wheeled in on a hospital bed, then two porters with well-practised efficiency slid her on to the bed and left. Rachel recognised the girl; she was the one who was being pushed out in a wheelchair with her leg in a splint, the one Kyle had stared at. Nothing happened for a while, the girl just lay motionless, still unconscious following her surgery, then the door opened, and two men walked in. They seemed to grin at each other and make shapes with their hands. Rachel wasn't sure why they were doing it until she realised that they were playing Rock, Paper, Scissors. The man who lost sat in the chair at the side of the bed and the other man stood at the opposite side. The man who was still standing had his back to the concealed camera, Rachel couldn't see his face, but he seemed to be touching the girl on the bed. After a while he climbed on top of her and then there was no doubt what he was doing.

'Who the hell is that!' She shouted to Kyle, but he wouldn't answer her.

Unwilling to watch, she fast-forwarded the tape until

the man was done, then as he clambered off, he turned away from the girl for some reason, perhaps shame, unknowingly facing the camera. Rachel hit pause and examined his face for a while, he looked familiar, but she couldn't quite place him.

Then it came to her. It was the porter who had been wheeling the girl out, the one who nodded to Kyle. She didn't need to see who the other man was; she knew instantly that it was Kyle.

'You sick bastards, how long have...' she started, then an icy chill ran down her spine.

Rachel stood up and studied the pile of tapes stacked on the shelf; there were dozens of them. She searched for one with her mother's name written on the label, but she couldn't see one. Relieved, she sank back into the chair, still looking up at the tapes.

'I didn't know,' Kyle said, staggering to his feet, 'didn't know he had put a camera there. Then one day he showed me a video of me doing... you know... and said he would post them on the Internet if I didn't do whatever he told me to do. I had no choice. Please, Rachel, get rid of them... I can't go to prison; you know happens to that sort of people in there.'

'Prisons too good for you - you fucking paedophile,' Steve said, as he ran forward to kick Kyle between the legs, causing him to double up in pain. Rachel didn't even look around; something was still bothering her about the tapes.

'What is it, Rach?' Steve asked, still looking down at Kyles crumpled form on the floor.

'There's no tape here with my mom's name on it, but I don't trust them not to have done anything...' her voice trailed off and she stood up to take another tape from the shelf.

'Damn,' she said, holding it up — it had the name Rachel written on it. She felt sick as she inserted the tape and pressed play.

It started in the same way as before with two people pushing a bed into the room. Rachel saw it was Kyle, but it was not the other porter who was with him this time, it was the doctor. The two men appeared to talk to each other for a moment, and then Rachel watched fascinated as she saw her mother moving and talking before Kyle passed something to the doctor. When he held his hand up, Rachel caught sight of the needle that he stuck into her mother's arm, and seconds later she saw her pass out on the bed. The doctor said something to Kyle then left him alone in the room with her.

When Rachel saw Kyle climb on top of her, she jabbed at the VCR ripping the cassette out and sat looking at it as if she had never seen one before in her life. Then she held it close against her chest. Steve looked at her unsure of what to do. Saying nothing, Rachel calmly put the cassette onto the table, took a needle from her pocket and roughly stuck it into Kyle's arm through his sleeve. Kyle looked up at her with a confused expression before his eyelids fluttered and slowly closed as he passed out.

'What the fuck Rach!'

'Shut up Steve I know what I'm doing.'

Steve was pacing, 'know what you are doing? Really because it looks like you just drugged somebody.'

'That *somebody* has abused my mother and God knows how many other people. You think I overreacted?' she said as she picked up the kitchen knife.

Rachel held it up in front of her face and looked at her reflection in its wide blade — she did not like what she saw. Steve saw Rachel frown, and in an instant, her face changed. It was only a subtle shift, and if you didn't know her, you might have missed it, but something was different now, she looked harder, more distant somehow.

Rachel nodded toward Kyle, 'come on, he won't be waking up any time soon. We'll drive back into the city, find a phone box and then report this to the police. They'll turn up find paedo-boy fast asleep and arrest the sick fuck.'

'What about fingerprints, DNA? We've touched things!' Steve exclaimed, frantically looking around the room.

Rachel put the knife down and pulled her sleeve over her hand and wiped the buttons on the VHS player.

'Relax Steve, you haven't touched anything,' she told him. Satisfied that the VHS player was clean, they made their way back out to Steve's car careful not to touch anything as they went. Steve closed the car door and breathed a sigh of relief as he looked over at Rachel, the tape with her name on it resting on her lap.

Steve started the car and put it into gear, and they drove away, keen to get away from this place.

'Stop! Stop the car!' She blurted out, opening her door and getting out before the vehicle had come to a complete standstill.

'I've left the knife in there — wait, I won't be long,' she said, running back toward the house.

The large knife looked out of place on the table next to the television.

Jesus that would have really screwed us if I left that she thought.

Rachel turned and looked at Kyle, pathetically curled up in the corner, his wrists still bound with packaging tape.

'Shit,' she muttered.

Rachel knelt and sawed away at the tape on his wrist until she cut through it. She tore the tape off, ripping the hairs from his wrist and as the tightness of the tape released, Kyles hands fell down by his side.

She looked at Kyles's face, he looked so peaceful, breathing softly in his deep sleep.

Rachel took out the remaining needles and injected their contents into Kyles arm, one by one.

With each injection, his breathing slowed, and his chest rose just a little less than before until finally, it rose no more.

CHAPTER FORTY-FOUR

Live Free or Die

'Take the back roads and then go north for a while Steve before we get back on the Highway,' Rachel said quietly.

Steve looked into the rear-view mirror, happy to see the house grow smaller and smaller until it disappeared completely as they headed towards the bridge.

He tried to slow the car as they reached it but not enough to stop the underside of the engine scraping against the old wood.

'Why, Rachel?'

Rachel clasped her hands together around the knife. 'Why what?'

'North', Steve said, glimpsing at the knife.

Rachel turned to look at him, 'what do you mean?'

'Why should we go north?'

It took a moment for her to understand his question before she answered.

'So it'll look like we've just carried on without taking a detour to the house, the traffic cameras on the

Highway would only see us leaving and then getting back on a little while after. We were in the house for what, about twenty minutes. Head towards Sandy Bay, we can turn back once we see the signs.'

They travelled in silence for a while, then Steve looked over and asked, 'why Sandy Bay?'

Rachel wound the window down, letting a blast of frigid air flood into the car.

'Oh, I don't know Steve, we wanted to see the ocean or something, but we had an argument and turned back before we got there. How does that sound?'

Steve frowned, 'okay, I guess.'

'Okay then, so that's what we'll say if anyone — even Kim asks. We'll say we couldn't find the house, so we dropped Kyle off near to a police station and left him there with the needles he shouldn't have. Only we'll know we went there.'

Rachel looked across at Steve, his mouth moving ever so slightly as he chewed his bottom lip.

'Why are you frowning Steve?'

'Just thinking about the time, you know if somebody tracked when we left the Highway and then got back on to it, there would be a block of time we would have to account for.'

'Right Steve,' Rachel said wearily, 'so we were heading to the coast for a romantic date, but we got too horny and had to find someplace to pull over and make out. That's why we left the Freeway for a while. How's that fucking sound!'

She took his silence for acceptance of the lies they would tell. They didn't talk or even look at each other until they reached the start of the Love Bridge over the Charles River. They slowed and eventually stopped in the heavy traffic clamouring to get through the city at the end of a working day. Boston had always seemed gloomy to Rachel, with its imposing buildings standing guard over the historic areas built hundreds of years ago by the founders of New England.

The dull winter afternoon made her feel oppressed; it felt as if the buildings were all leaning in toward her, judging her. Rachel's eyes locked onto the new brickwork at the end of the bridge, repaired only days after her mother and Josh had left the road in the very same place. Images of traffic cones flying and scattering in all directions as the car hit them filled her mind. She was jolted back to the present by Steve's voice.

'I'll go to a car wash after I take you home. Make sure that there's no soil and things from around the area of the house.'

Rachel looked through the windscreen at a 'Live Free or Die' bumper sticker on the car in front and without looking at Steve, she shook her head, wondering what the hell she had gotten them into.

A police car with sirens blazing crawled through the web of vehicles towards their car. Steve shot a glance at Rachel, who couldn't have looked more suspicious if she tried.

'It can't be, can it Rach - they can't have found him yet — could they?'

'Not unless someone saw us, there wasn't anyone there, the place was deserted.' Rachel answered, although paranoia set in when the police car passed them, and one of the police officers looked straight at her.

This is it she thought. Murder. I've killed him, and they know - they can tell when someone is guilty just by looking at them, they're trained for it.

As much as she wanted to, she couldn't break off her stare. The police officer frowned and spoke into the mic strapped to his chest without looking away from Rachel.

Reporting me, checking my description, making sure it's me before they arrest me.

And suddenly a gap opened in the traffic and the police car untangled itself and sped past them and was soon lost from view.

Rachel was on edge for the rest of the journey, convinced that everybody was watching her. The shoppers waiting at the traffic lights next to Quincy market stared into the car when Steve stopped to let them cross the road. Shortly after they turned onto Tremont Street and saw the graveyard tour guide in his traditional costume sneaking a smoke between tours. He looked at Rachel as he ground his cigarette stub into the ground. Rachel was sure the firemen outside the station even stopped what they were doing to watch. She even thought Steve was looking at her suspiciously from the corner of his eye.

When they pulled up outside her house, Rachel practically leapt from the car and rushed to it, almost losing her footing as she slipped on the steps. She closed the door and stood with her back to it.

Kim sat at the kitchen table, picking at the crust of a half-eaten pizza when Rachel stormed in interrupting her social media browsing.

Rachel hesitated for a moment when she saw Kim in the kitchen and not sat next to her mother.

As if sensing her thoughts, Kim stood up and announced, 'Rach, I was just taking a break. She hasn't woken up, not even moved at all really.'

Rachel ignored Kim and knelt down next to her mother, staring at her face, searching for any signs showing that she knew she was there. There was a slight wheezing noise as her chest rose and fell, and Rachel noticed a vein in her mother's neck throb steadily, beads of sweat glistened on her forehead.

'Thanks, Kim, Steve will take you home - I've told him to wait outside for you.'

'Hang on Rach. I'm not sure you should be on your own right now.'

Rachel didn't turn to look at Kim, 'It's okay Kim, to be honest, I could just do with a little peace and quiet now, it's been a very, very, long day if you know what I mean.'

'Okay - I'll call you tomorrow,' Kim said, before pausing and turning at the door to ask, 'where's Kyle?'

Rachel didn't answer and only realised that she had been holding her breath when she heard Kim gently close the door behind her.

CHAPTER FORTY-FIVE
Cold Case

Rachel felt the tingling sensation in her legs, as pins and needles started to arrive. She gripped the arm of the sofa and groaned as she rose up. Rachel felt dog-tired. She stamped her feet to kick start the blood-flow in her legs before shuffling into the kitchen to pick up a cloth to dry her mother's brow. When Rachel came back, she noticed her mother had shifted slightly on the sofa.

That's a positive sign, she must be waking up Rachel thought, dabbing her mother's brow gently with the cloth, half expecting her to wake up. But she didn't.

Rachel paused, staring at her face sunk into the cream coloured cushion, wondering what she would look like in a coffin, cold and lifeless. Kyles face flashed across her thoughts, dragging her deep into a dark place in her mind's eye.

She wondered what it would be like to be in a coffin, six foot underground - but not dead. She closed her eyes and instantly her mind took her there. In the absolute blackness Rachel's heart beat a loud tattoo, she clawed at the lid, fingernails digging into the wood, scratching and scraping. Nails cracked; wood splinters stabbed her fingertips. Rachel was consumed by the blackness; the scratching of wood grew louder and louder until a noise yanked her from her trance.

She turned towards the sound; the dog barked again then resumed his scratching at the door.

'Cujo!'

Rachel opened the door slowly, Cujo brushed past her heading straight to his food bowl, turning to offer Rachel an accusing stare. She filled his bowl, and the old dog gulped his food down almost instantly.

'Good boy,' Rachel said, stroking his long fur which has brought the cold in with it.

She watched the dog for a while, wondering when the day all pet owner dread would come - it's always sooner than you think. As she watched Cujo, Rachel slipped her hands in her pockets, her mind racing about what she has done. Killed someone, killed Kyle. Her wrist demanded attention, and as she starts to claw at it something stops her, Rachel notices that she's broken a fingernail somehow, the tip of her finger bleeding from a small cut.

'Odd,' she says aloud, before sucking on her finger and staring at her motionless mother on the sofa.

Rachel crept past, so she didn't wake her and felt ridiculous as she did so, because that's precisely what she wanted to happen. She even avoided the creaking step as she continued up to her room.

Rachel sat on her bed for a moment thinking about the last time she saw Josh, waving at her from the back of the car.

The police told her that he might have been swept downriver, perhaps her mother had gotten Josh out of the car first and wasn't it lucky that some off-duty medical staff saw the vehicle leave the road.

Not long after the crash, the police told her to register Josh's details on the NamUs, missing person database; despite over six hundred thousand people going missing each year it was worth a try they said. But so far there were no hits on his profile or anyone vaguely matching Josh's description. She closed her eyes to clear her head, but when she did, she was transported straight back to that house, finding herself staring down at Kyle's lifeless body. Rachel needed to do something to distract her from what she'd done and to keep Kyle at bay and who knows, perhaps now her mother was back things might be looking positive for once.

She picked up the laptop and pressed the power button waking the computer from its slumber to whir into life. Rachel stared down at her wet sneakers as the laptop seemed to take an age to start up, as things do when you are in a hurry. Rachel picked at the tip of her cut finger until the laptop finished its start-up routine, finally showing a screen filled with a mass of folders arranged in no particular order.

She opened a browser window and typed in the address for NamUs and read the websites depressing opening message:

"Over 600,000 individuals go missing in the United States every year. Fortunately, many missing children and adults are quickly found, alive and well. However, tens of thousands of

individuals remain missing for more than one year – what many agencies consider "cold cases."

She scrolled down to read:

"It is estimated that 4,400 unidentified bodies are recovered each year, with approximately 1,000 of those bodies remaining unidentified after one year."

Rachel closed her eyes and sighed. When she opened them, she looked down at the keys on her laptop; they were smeared with blood from her finger. She looked at herself in the mirror, the light casting harsh shadows over her face accentuating the hollows of her eyes and cheeks. Rachel felt her cheeks become damp as the tears she had been holding in flowed. She wiped them away and then as if on autopilot, went to the bathroom to look for a band-aid.

She closed the bathroom door and rested her back against it standing there as if in a stupor waiting for her eyes to adjust to the dimness as the low energy light bulb warmed up. Rachel felt for her crucifix on her necklace, her fingers tracing over the edges of the cross; pressing the sharp edges into her skin.

Finally, it was light enough to see, Rachel shook her head as she looked around at the peeling wallpaper and spots of mould which had formed in the corners of the room above the small window. As the light grew brighter, a couple of cockroaches paused as if irritated by the interruption, their antennae making random motions, trying to seek out the source of their invasion. Rachel stamped on one, enjoying the squelching noise of its death under her sneaker. As if realising it was next, the remaining cockroach made a hasty zig-zagging escape under the washing basket.

'I hate these things.' She said aloud. The crushed cockroach waved its antennae in response as its yellow innards oozed out of its body onto the bathroom floor. Rachel rested her hands on the sink and closed her eyes, taking in a sharp intake of breath before raising her head to look at the reflection in the grubby mirror of the bathroom cabinet.

Her face stared mockingly back at her; a little duller, deader than the last time she had looked at herself. Rachel sighed as she opened the bathroom cupboard to look for a band-aid, but there were none; it was practically empty except for a few half-used toothpaste tubes, a bar of soap and a pair of scissors. Rachel took the scissors by the handles, opening them wide to expose their sharp edges, then turned the palm of her left hand to the ceiling in a motion that looked like she was waiting to be handed her change from shopping.

'Forgive me, Josh,' she whispered as she pressed the cold, sharp metal into her wrist.

CHAPTER FORTY-SIX

Like mother, like daughter

'What the fuck am I thinking!' she snarled at the scissors and dropped them into the sink.

'Damn it!' Rachel looked around the bathroom for a towel to wipe the new wound on her wrist with, but she couldn't see one.

Blood ran down her arm as she picked up the washing basket to shake the contents out. As the pile of dirty clothes tumbled out, a bottle hit the floor with a thud. Rachel picked it up and stared at the clear liquid behind the Seagrams Vodka label before twisting off the cap and taking a swig, coughing as the alcohol burned her throat and empty stomach. The second taste wasn't as bad and well, as the third mouthful went down the comfort of alcohol began to take over.

Rachel kicked the pile of clothes over to the door, forming them into a makeshift pillow and sank down onto them and started drinking in earnest, emptying the bottle surprisingly quickly.

'Cheers, mom,' she slurred, as the room began to spin uncomfortably. Rachel didn't like it, she closed her eyes, but that was even worse. She decided to go back to her bedroom, but when she tried standing the world tilted on its axis, and she thought better of it, falling to her knees as her legs betrayed her.

'Fuck.'

Rachel managed to get on her hands and knees; the only thing on her mind was to reach the bedroom. She reached up for the door handle, struggling to pull it open as clothes snagged under it and was about to give up on the idea when she heard her mobile phone buzzing, reverberating loudly on the table, dragging her attention to it. Rachel pulled the door open a crack, then with two hands yanked it half-open, slid through and staggered on to her room.

The phone's screen was still bright when she got there, and Rachel strained and snatched at it, her actions out of sync with her thoughts, but somehow, she managed to reach the phone; but then it slithered out of her hand, falling to the floor. Rachel dropped to her knees and without her body warning her, vomited and fell headfirst into her own sticky mess. The phone continued to ring mockingly. Her breath was hot on her face as she inhaled the warmth of the sick back into her mouth, panicking that she was about to suffocate, she summoned all the strength she had left to turn her head to the side. As her eyes flickered shut, before the blackness came, she caught sight of Kim's smirking face staring at her from the screen of the mobile phone.

It was the smell Rachel noticed first. She tried to open her eyes, but one wouldn't - vomit had dried over it and sealed it shut. Rachel rubbed it until the seal broke with a slight crack. Small pieces of vomit clung to her eyelashes and scratched her eyes when she blinked. She scrambled onto her hands and knees, staring blankly at the patch of vomit with its odd smell. There was something else. Rachel slowly reached between her legs and fought the urge to vomit again when she felt the dampness there. She struggled to stand. It seemed like the world was rushing up around her, so Rachel decided to crawl out of her room. Near the door, Rachel saw her mobile phone, the picture of Kim that she had added to her contact details looked up at her. Thirteen missed calls, the last one almost two hours ago.

It seemed to take an eternity to crawl back to the bathroom, her fingers struggling to grip on the musty carpet. The light seemed different on the landing, casting strange, unfamiliar shadows on the wall. To Rachel, they appeared to be out of sync with her movements as if they weren't really shadows at all, but something else following her, perhaps Kyle's spirit. Down there on the floor crawling like a dog, Rachel didn't dare look at the shadows again.

In the bathroom, Rachel struggled into a sitting position in the shower and reached up to twist the tap, releasing the spray of water. It was ice-cold, but she didn't care, it was the most real thing happening at the moment for Rachel. As it soaked through her clothes, a puddle formed around her before it found its way to the plug hole. As Rachel watched it trickle through the clumps of hair caught in the plughole, she began to cry.

PART THREE

COLD METAL BURNS

CHAPTER FORTY-SEVEN

2

People aren't born to live; people are born to die. Think about it, from the moment you arrive into this world with nothing, you are slowly dying. I used to think I was a strong person, a rock, somebody for other people to rely on or look up to. But I'm not. When I get to thinking about it I don't suppose that anybody is strong, we are all just existing, drifting from day to day denying the inevitable slow creep of age pulling us all to our graves. Many people realise their own mortality sometime before their midlife crisis causing them to buy new things, a new car, new hair and teeth, a new wife, that sort of thing, but I realised that I was not going to live forever when I was a small boy. It was in one of those never-ending summers between school terms where you would call for your friends in the morning and return home tired and dirty knee'd in the early evening; or whenever you heard your mother shouting you. How did they do that? It didn't matter how far away you were, you always heard them.

Anyway, I'd come home early and was drinking a lukewarm homemade banana milkshake that still had lumps of powder floating around in it when my mother came in looking all sad. Turns out that my little dog Ben had been run over by a bus. Did I want to look at him before my dad buried him in the back garden she asked? I shook my head, I was not in the mood to see a dead friend, animal or otherwise and went back to drinking and chewing my milkshake.

And that's when the rock of my life started to be chipped steadily away; dead pets, dead relationships, parents passing away; and then your circle of friends slowly decreasing until you end up sitting all alone like a rock surrounded piles of stone fragments, each piece representing something that once mattered to you.

But there are so many pieces. And even if you could put the jigsaw of your life back together would you want to make all the pieces fit this time?

CHAPTER FORTY-EIGHT
Unravelling

It was Saturday and Rachel was up early as she was so often these days. She had never been a morning person, but with Josh missing, she wanted to be up in case he came home. But he never did. Cujo was curled up in the middle of the living room, head resting against the repaired leg of the coffee table, his paws twitching as he chased something in his dreams. Rachel remembered tossing the table around the room, recalled it smashing against the wall where they discovered the box. That fucking box. The damn box must have been cursed because everything went from bad to worse when she opened it. It was like opening a can of worms that slithered out and infected everything they touched. Cujo's paws stopped moving then he let out a whimper and continued his chase.

I wish I could chase away my dreams, Rachel thought. The dog's ribs rose and fell, and she could see the bones of his rib cage as he breathed - Kyle still breathed in her dreams. Rachel had a recurring dream where he stopped breathing after she injected the drugs into his bloodstream. She had done this, of course, but in her dreams, he always opened his eyes and looked at her, standing up, tearing the needles from his arm and tossing them aside. His eyes were always vacant, lifeless like somebody had poured bleach into them, making them translucent. When he looked at her, she could see no difference in the colour of his pupils and the yellowed whites of his eyes. He would start in a crouch and uncoil himself as he stood up. In the dreams, he was much bigger and stronger than in real life. He would grab hold of her wrists and hold them above her head, pinning her against the wall. She could feel his dirty, broken nails sink deep into her skin and sometimes when she woke up, there were cuts in her wrists and blood on the sheets. Rachel told herself that she had done it in her sleep, but in that time in the dead of the night, before you fully wake up, she wasn't so sure.

The morning quiet was soon interrupted by a steadily increasing number of cars passing by, and the bang and clattering from a nearby construction site. Rachel turned the thermostat up: the house had always been cold, but since Josh had gone, it seemed so much colder. Soon the noise of the old radiators fought against the sound of the music seeping through the wall from the house next door. It was hard to make out the lyrics, but it was easy to make out when the needle caught in a scratch on the vinyl record making it skip and repeat the same line over and over again. Probably some hipster had moved in and thought they were too cool for MP3, or maybe they were actually old people who couldn't be bothered to catch up with technology.

There was a small pop, and the room suddenly became a little darker when one of the lightbulbs died. Rachel glanced at it momentarily, and when she looked away, she could see a blob of light wherever she looked for a while. In the strange new light, Rachel could see slight imperfections in the walls where pictures had once hung, now the space was bare, the screw holes were filled but stood out slightly in the shadows. Imperfections hiding in plain sight. Like her.

For a few days after coming home, Rachel's mother couldn't remember much of her ordeal in the hospital. Her recovery was as unspectacular as they come - she simply woke up one morning, said she was starving and asked for some food. The crash seemed the hardest thing for her to remember and caused her to withdraw into herself when asked any direct questions about it. The only thing she would say is that everything went dark and then she woke up in the back of somebody else's car. It didn't make sense. Rachel suspected that she remembered more than she was letting on and pressed as much as she dared. But how do you do that without pretty much accusing her of killing Josh? She took to spending most of the day in her room, Rachel tried her best to look after her, often finding that her mother hadn't eaten any of the food that she had taken up.

Once, about a week after her return home, Rachel went to her room to collect another tray of uneaten food and had heard her talking about a gun as she tossed and turned in a fitful sleep. Rachel intended to ask her about it when she woke up later, but she'd never seen a gun in the house or anywhere else for that matter, except for the toy one from the Cowboys and Indians play set that she had bought Josh a few days before the crash.

She could picture him now in the car, aiming the big plastic gun at her as she launched arrows back at the windows, their suction cups making them stick briefly to the glass. Rachel remembered Josh grinning back at her as he looked down the barrel of the big silver toy gun before excitedly pulling the trigger. Perhaps that was the one she was dreaming about Rachel thought; maybe she had played the same game with Josh.

Her mother's face had always been thin, but now, as she had come to accept Josh's absence, it had taken on a terribly severe look. Her skin had an ashen appearance which caused her cheekbones to stand out more, and her dark-ringed eyes now held a sorrow which never left them.

She was still not up to leaving the house, but Rachel was glad to see her up and about and pleased that she had started to clear up after herself. Rachel would still take food up each morning, but now her mother would bring down the tray of empty plates later in the day, and she had started to shower again which was a good sign. Still unwilling to accept what had happened to her wasn't a fiction of her imagination, her mother would often ask where Josh was - until the crushing realisation hit moments later.

Today seemed like a good day for her mother, though. Rachel had heard her get up, shower, and when she came downstairs into the living room, Rachel noticed that she had clean clothes on and had fixed her hair and make-up.

'Hungry mom?'

'No, I'm good Rach,' she replied, settling onto the sofa.

She fished out the remote control from under a cushion and pressed the power button to switch the TV on. The light from it lit up and dimmed the room as the images on it changed. Rachel eyed her mother, anxiously.

'Want to watch a movie or something?' Rachel suggested.

'No, I just want the noise, helps me to stop thinking about… you know.' She said as she thumbed up the volume then set the control on the table.

Cujo raised his head to regard them both suspiciously before settling back down. Rachel sat next to her mom, and they both watched a breakfast cereal advertisement end and a news bulletin begin.

The faces of the newscasters were serious. The woman glanced down at her notes and frowned. A picture of Kyle in his hospital uniform, presumably from his ID badge, appeared behind her on the screen.

'What the fu…' Rachel started.

'Rach? Did you say something?'

'No,' her voice barely a whisper.

The male newscaster spoke. 'An investigation carried out by the Boston Globe newspaper has unearthed a culture of abuse at Boston General Hospital. You might remember that the Boston Globe also brought to light the scandal of abuse in the Catholic church in 2002.'

The female newscaster nodded in affirmation and then took over the narrative.

'Although the police won't comment on an active

investigation, it is believed that the body of Kyle Kennedy, reported missing by his parents several weeks ago, has been recovered after being discovered by construction workers. His body was found by workers when they began clearing the area in preparation to renovate the location into the long-awaited dam which will supply the greater Boston area.'

Rachel clenched her fists as she watched wide-eyed as the image on the screen changed to the house in Dog Town, where she had killed Kyle. Police tape fluttered in the breeze around the perimeter of the house, and a body in a sealed body-bag was wheeled out to a waiting ambulance.

The male newscaster took over again. 'Sources in the Boston Globe claim to have video evidence of Kennedy and other members of the hospital staff sexually abusing patients, some as young as 12 years old.'

Rachel felt her mother reach for her hand as the video ended and was replaced with a stock image of the hospital.

The male newscaster continued, 'the Boston Globe allege that they have it on good authority that Kennedy commuted suicide, perhaps out of shame for what he did to those poor patients.'

Rachel chewed the inside of her cheek tasting blood; thoughts of armed police kicking her door down and arresting her flooding her mind. She looked at her mother out of the corner of her eye and saw her staring straight ahead at the screen.

'Police are urging anyone who had an operation over the past year to contact their physician. They are also appealing for anyone with information on the whereabouts of this man, going by the name of Dr Ayden Massey, to call them immediately.'

A grainy, full-body CCTV image of the doctor appeared on the screen.

The female newscaster continued, '… and in other news, the Boston Red Sox are hoping to finish the season with…'

Rachel saw her lips moving but was no longer hearing the words, and when she turned to look at her mother, they both burst into tears.

CHAPTER FORTY-NINE

Kisses and Make Up

'Jesus, Rach why do you never clean your room?' Kim said, scooping up a tangled mass of clothes from the bed and holding them up.

'Rach?'

'What?'

Kim scanned the two different piles of clothes on the floor, 'so erm, which pile?'

'Whatever Kim - if it smells okay, put it on the one under the window, if not throw it in the corner'.

Kim threw all of the clothes into the corner, 'Rachel, that's gross - I'm not sniffing your clothes.'

Rachel opened the lid of her laptop and waited for Kim to come over. They both squeezed onto the chair and waited for it to finish starting up. Kim noticed that one of the corners of the laptop was dented and some of the keys were missing. She began to ask about it but thought better of it.

'So, I thought we could do like a sort of a cross between Freddy Kruger and a skeleton, what do reckon Rachel?' Kim held up two red and black striped sweaters she'd picked up from a thrift store.

Rachel nodded and replied, 'Kruger, retro. But I like it.'

'Okay, so you make some cuts in them, and then I'll smear this fake blood over them,' she said, passing the scissors to Kim. When they finished cutting and painting the jumpers with blood, they pulled them on and looked each other up and down.

'Great, now let's Google some skeleton faces,' Rachel said. As she started to type, a chat window popped open showing Steve's smiling face.

'Not now Steve, we're far too busy,' Kim announced as she steered the mouse to the corner of the chat screen to unceremoniously cut him off.

'Hey, why did you do that?

Kim flashed an annoyed look at Rachel, 'well, it's supposed to be our thing isn't it Rach? Remember all those month's when your mom was in the hospital and we'd talk about how good it would be to do the tourist things around Boston? When we'd plan what to wear and where to go. Anyway, you owe me some Rach-time after all the times you bailed on me to spend time with him. Or have you forgotten...'

Rachel cut in, 'no, of course I haven't Kim, you have been amazing. All the times in the hospital, and the support you have given me these last few months as my mom is getting back to something like she used to be - I couldn't have done it without you. I mean that.'

'Right, and she did say it would make her happy for us to do this, didn't she?'

Rachel nodded.

'Okay then, let's get on with it.' Kim said, returning to

the computer screen.

Kim was right of course, Rachel thought, Steve had been so helpful, and she'd gotten to know him really well over the last few months. But after spending a lot of time with him, Rachel realised there was no romantic attraction at all. He was a nice guy and all that, but the spark was missing. Kim had warned her that he'd want something in return for his help and although she wouldn't admit it, Rachel thought that she might be right.

Rachel was waiting to tell him to back off a little but didn't know how he'd take the let's just be friend's speech. Not too well, she expected - they never did. She remembered when she broke up with Jamie Jackson. He was her first true love, and at the time they were the couple everybody thought would be together forever. It began to go downhill when he started posting pictures of himself with other girls, just as a joke he'd said when she saw them. This wasn't very pleasant, and after a bit of warranted snooping around his room one evening, Rachel found a second cell phone. But try as she might she couldn't unlock it, so she just put it back where she had found it and left. At first, Jamie was puzzled at why he'd been dumped him without warning and crept around Rachel for weeks; buying flowers and gifts and promising her the world.

Steve's voice snapped Rachels attention back to the laptop screen.

'So, don't mind me girls - I'll just watch you get ready,' his voice sounded tinny as it came through the speakers on the laptop.

Almost in perfect synchronicity, they flipped him the bird then Rachel leaned in to close the chat window, 'bye-bye,' she said with a consoling smile.

Kim searched the internet, 'okay, so let's find a tutorial on YouTube.' After a little while, they settled on making their faces up like skeletons but only on one side so that when they put their faces close to one another, it made one skeleton's face - sort of.

Rachel picked up her phone, and they stood close together and clicked away to capture some selfies. After ten shots in various states of pout, Rachel tossed the phone onto the bed.

'C'mon Kim, are you ready? Let's go.'

After a final check in the mirror, they left the room and seconds later the webcam came back on, and Steve appeared in the small chat window. He shouted hello and waved. If anyone was in the room to see him, they would have seen his disappointment. Steve was about to disconnect when he spotted a Freddy Kruger-cum-Skeleton enter the room.

'Wow, Rachel you look amazing, listen where will you be later tonight?'

Steve saw the skeleton's face move close to the screen and saw her put a finger to her mouth signalling him to be quiet.

'Give me a twirl Rach - you look great.'

She spun around slowly, showing off her body. Steve was enjoying the sight of the ripped woollen sweater, which occasionally flashed glimpses of her white lace bra. He was looking at her ripped fishnet stockings when he saw her stop and begin slowly lifting up her top, showing off her stomach. She hears Steve start talking excitedly and she reaches forward to put him on mute. Staring straight at him, she pulls the sweater over her head and then stands with her hands-on-hips almost defiantly, but it was not her eyes that Steve was looking at.

'Have you found it,' came the shout from downstairs. She closed the laptop lid, pulled on her sweater then straightened up her clothes before picking the phone up from the bed.

'Yes, Rachel - coming now,' Kim shouted back.

CHAPTER FIFTY
The Freedom Trail?

Having seen the State House, the monument for the
African-American soldiers and the site of the Boston
Massacre, Rachel and Kim walked through Boston
Common and found themselves standing outside of the
Granary Burial Ground.

Rachel shuddered, remembering the last time she'd
passed by the graveyard, not long after killing Kyle.
Rachel peered unhappily into the cemetery trying to
remember who was buried in there: Samuel Adams,
John Hancock and Robert someone or other were in
there, as well as about 5000 other people. Some were
lucky enough to have their own gravestones, but many
had been reburied and shared their graves with strangers.
The word 'intertwined' came to mind.

'What's wrong?' said Kim.

'Nothing, I was just thinking about all these graves,'
she replied, turning to face her friend.

Kim looked at the row nearest to her, most of them had
some sort of winged skull or a ship carved into the top of

the headstone. Shovels, sandbags and various tools lay near to a grave of someone important which was in the middle of being renovated.

'What about them?'

'Well some of these graves have two or three bodies in them - look at that one over there, that's got five bodies in it. I was just thinking about when they start to rot and decompose. I suppose their bodies sort of mix together and seep into the ground.'

'That's gross,' said Kim.

'I know, right? Imagine if you believed in reincarnation and came back to life in the future as a mix of these people? Maybe if you were a good person in this life you might come back as a murderer or something. Some people believe that you come back as animals, you know?' She added.

'Well I'm just glad that we are good Catholic girls who will definitely be going to heaven,' said Kim making the sign of the cross before genuflecting.

'Amen to that,' laughed Rachel.

'Come on, let's head back down to Quincy to get a drink.' Kim pointed to the Starbucks sign attached to a lamppost, pointing roughly in the direction of the indoor market. Once a trading post for goods as exciting as eggs and flour, in recent times Quincy Market has become a natural resting stop for people following the Freedom Trail.

'Okay, cool, let's go' replied Rachel after one last look into the graveyard.

It didn't matter what time of day it was, the cemetery always seemed dark and cold, almost as if the people buried there were sucking any scrap of heat. After a short walk back through Boston Common, skirting around the drunks and drug addicts, they came to the main road and waited for the traffic lights to change so they could cross.

Above the entrance to the indoor market, two American flags hung limply, and below them, a banner flapping slowly in the light breeze proclaimed, 'Happy Halloween!'

A pair of spotlights beamed their bright light up to illuminate the banner making it cast strange shadows as it moved. The air had a cool feel to it, but this hadn't put people off dressing up for the occasion, and they watched a group of Harvard undergrads dressed as various 'scary' monsters conga-dance over the road in front of them.

'Jeez, look at the state of her!' said Kim nodding towards a woman dressed as a cheerleader with her face painted to look like it had been slashed down one side of it.

'Why what's wrong with her?' Rachel asked, 'it's a really good costume.'

'It sure is. Look, you can nearly see her ass under that stupid little skirt every time she congas.'

'Oh, I see... wait, oh I really do see!' Rachel said as the 'dead' cheerleader's skirt rode up as she bounced in time with her dance.

Laughing, Kim and Rachel crossed the road and headed towards the wide plaza area in front of the market. A large crowd had gathered to watch an athletic-looking street performer called 'Andre' show off his dance moves before asking for a dollar for his efforts.

'This is the dance I did on Americas Got Talent,' he announced over his microphone before launching into his well-practised sequence of moves ending with a backflip; the crowd cheered and reached for their dollars.

'He's good isn't' he,' said Rachel, 'let's watch for a while.'

'It's getting a bit cold but sure, let's sit here,' Kim pointed to a long concrete bench where there was space next to a group of bored-looking British exchange students. As they sat, Rachel looked around and saw about thirty of them interspersed in the crowd clearly identifiable by the maroon hoodies that they wore. What she didn't notice was the man who had been following them for hours move into the shadows behind them.

'And for my next trick I'll need some volunteers,' the street performer yelled into his microphone.

Rachel smiled as most of the crowd seemed to look away from his gaze or decide to look for something in their bags. A tall, thin young Asian man was 'volunteered' by his girlfriend with an encouraging push, and the street performer quickly changed the CD track to 'Gangnam Style' and began dancing with the man who gamely joined in.

'You're so Asian!' Andre said, once the track had finished, the man smiling as if not fully understanding how unpolitical correct the statement was.

'Now I need somebody who is a little bit wider,' he said, and he began skipping around the gathered circle until he found his next victim.

This came in the form of a rather large Italian looking man who was around 6ft 2 tall and looked like he weighed around 300 lbs. His slicked back black hair caught the light as he moved to the centre of the plaza unsure of his fate. He was wearing a pair of light coloured chinos and a black leather jacket that has been zipped up to the neck to keep out the cold and in the right light he wouldn't be out of place in a gangster movie. A real wise guy.

'One more! I need one more,' the street performer shouted as he spun around on the balls of his feet. A young boy, not much older than 10 years old skipped into the middle of the circle, turned around and bowed to his parents, who were recording his actions through their mobile phones. Hearing the crowd laugh he repeated his bow once more before the Andre grabbed him by his newly purchased '612 Boston Strong' hoodie and pulled him towards his other volunteers.

As if suddenly realising that he actually didn't like being in front of a crowd, the boy nervously stroked his spikey blond hair and looked down at his sneakers as he was informed that he was going to be jumped over while standing fully upright.

Andre skipped around in front of his audience clapping his hands shouting 'Andre, Andre Andre,' until the crowd joined in. He lined himself up with his target and ran towards the increasingly worried looking boy whose shoulders had slumped down in a feeble attempt to make himself smaller. Andre bounced in front of the boy, leapt into the air, and landed just in front of the crowd, his dreadlocks spilling down over his face.

'Wow!' Kim said, looking at Rachel, who turned to her and nodded her agreement. From the corner of her eye, Rachel caught sight of movement in the shadows near to the building behind them.

The man saw her look directly at him and froze in place, remaining absolutely still, confident that his black clothing and the shadows would safely conceal him.

'What's up?' said Kim, annoyed that she didn't have the full attention of her friend. Rachel turned to look at her before turning to look back at the corner of the building.

'I thought I saw something over there,' she said, nodding towards the dark corner. Seeing that Rachel had turned to speak to her friend, the man saw his chance and moved a little further back into the shadows, making himself invisible to their stares.

'I can't see anything, Rachel you're just getting a little jumpy because it's Halloweeeeeen and the dead can walk the earth!' Kim said, changing the tone of her voice in a terrible attempt at a spooky accent.

'Maybe you're right,' replied Rachel, but she couldn't help glancing back towards the corner, unsettled by the feeling of being watched.

The moon was growing fuller in the sky, and the steady breeze suddenly turned itself into an intense but short-lived gust of wind. The hairs on the back of Rachel's neck stood up, but this had nothing to do with the change in temperature.

Rachel looked at Kim, 'come on let's go inside, I'm cold and need to pee,' she urged.

Kim shook her head as she watched the street performer set fire to the end of his juggling clubs.

'No, you go, I want to watch. Based on his past efforts, this could go spectacularly wrong - just grab me a latte or something on the way out will you.'

'Okay, just stay right here?' Rachel said with a quick glance to the corner.

'Sure, I'll be here Rach.'

Rachel skirted around the edge of the crowd until she reached the wide steps leading up to the indoor market. She stood next to one of the four thick pillars and peered inside; the food merchants handed over cheap snacks to witches, zombies and the occasional vampire. The bustle reminded Rachel of an ant's nest as people pushed past each other to get their food.

I wish Kim had come with me, she thought as she walked into the nest. Rachel felt oppressed by the low ceiling, the narrow aisles and the writhing wall of people; her wrist ached for attention. Rachel shuffled slowly through the crowd, ignoring the shouts from the food vendors telling her that they had the best crab chowder, authentic Italian street food and whatever else until it just became a blur of noise buzzing around inside her head.

CHAPTER FIFTY-ONE

Gatherings

Rachel finally reached the toilets, and after finishing, she sat for a while listening to the meaningless conversations and babbling of gossip outside of her toilet stall. Once she was sure that she was alone, Rachel left the stall and looked at herself in the mirror as she washed her hands.

I should be at home with mom instead of wasting my time here, she thought, turning away from the mirror.

She found herself looking down at a wall-mounted hand dryer that professed to be, 'Fast, Clean and Hygienic' but it was none of these, and it certainly wasn't quiet. In fact, it was loud enough to mask the sound of the man dressed in black who had been following her all night, enter the toilets.

The man pulled his 'Friday the 13th' Jason mask up until it rested on the top of his head then he grabbed Rachel by her shoulders.

'Jesus, Steve! What the hell are you doing in here? Get out.' She shouted over the rattling din of the hand dryer. He laughed as he pressed himself against her, pinning her to the wall, Rachel could feel his arousal.

A smell of alcohol came with his words, 'thought we'd finish what we started earlier,' he grinned at her.

'Get off me Steve, what the hell are you doing!?' Her words surprisingly loud now the dryer had cut out.

Rachel pushed against his shoulders, but he was too strong for her.

'C'mon Rach,' he slurred as he leaned forward to kiss her.

Rachel pulled her head backwards and shoved at his chest, moving him slightly, making him press against the button of the hand dryer, forcing it noisily back to life.

'What are you talking about, get the fuck off me Steve!'

He pressed himself harder against her, 'what are you talking about,' he answered back, trying to imitate Rachel's voice.

'You've been leading me on for months now, flirting with me - and then, and then tonight you more or less told me I could have you! So don't try to get out of it now. Come on, let's go into one of those stalls.'

He grabbed her by the shoulders and forced her back towards an empty cubicle. As he did so, Rachel's feet got tangled with his, and she fell backwards hitting her face on the edge a sink. Blood ran into her eye from the cut on the left side of her face, and she found herself on the cold tiled floor looking up at Steve.

'Shit, Rachel I'm...' He started to say something, but his words were interrupted when the door burst open, and three giggling witches walked in. Before they could take in what had happened, Steve pulled down his mask and barged past them.

'Hey, watch it, asshole!' the nearest witch asked as she stepped forward to help Rachel up.

'Are you alright?' the witch asked.

'Shall I get the police?' another one of the witches said.

'No, no I'm fine,' Rachel replied, gingerly touching the cut by her eye and wincing.

'Looks nasty, might need stitches. Come on we'll take you.'

'No! It's fine, my friend will take me; she's just outside.'

One of the witches took off her black glove, ran it under the tap and handed it to Rachel.

'Here, keep this pressed on it until you get there.'

Rachel pressed it tight against the cut and nodded a thank you to the coven and then left the toilets to fight her way out of the ant's nest back to Kim outside.

But when she made it outside, Kim was nowhere to be seen.

CHAPTER FIFTY-TWO
The Moon

Kim wasn't there. Rachel looked around but couldn't see her in the thinning crowd, so she decided to walk back to the spot where Kim's father had dropped them off earlier.

God knows why we decided to do this, we should have thought ahead and arranged to get picked up at Quincy, Rachel muttered to herself as she set off past Faneuil Hall, keeping to the lit areas as much as she could.

Rachel took the long way around Boston Common so as not to aggravate any of its intoxicated residents, which meant she had to go past the graveyard again. When Rachel had passed it earlier, it seemed a bit creepy in the way they all are, but Kim had been with her then. They'd even cracked a few jokes with the costumed tour guides who were milling around handing out leaflets.

Now, as she looked in over the low wall, the old gravestones reminded her of rows of dirty crooked teeth grinning menacingly up at the moon. Even the moon thousands of miles away seemed intimidated and tried to hide behind a passing cloud before being subjected again

to the never-changing grin. It was getting close to
midnight now, the witching hour, and Rachel was
beginning to feel uneasy with easy passing minute. The
road passing the graveyard was quiet, as everybody had
headed down to the market area. Rachel pulled out her
phone to call Kim, and when she unlocked the screen,
there were 15 missed calls from Steve, just seeing his
name made her shiver.

Kim's face smiled back at her brightly as she pulled up
her contact details, but Rachel she swore as the call
failed, there was no signal, and the battery was nearly
dead too.

She strolled on, holding the phone in the air to try to
pick up reception. Before she knew it, she had walked
the length of the wall and had stopped by the graveyard
gates as the screen on her phone finally picked up a faint
signal. She was about to dial Kim's number when she
caught sight of something moving just behind the gates.
When she turned to get a better look, it was no longer
there; maybe it was a dog or a city fox, and she'd scared
it away.

It started to rain, the fine misty type that gets you
quickly soaked to the skin and Rachel could already feel
it beginning to wash away the makeup from her face.
Rachel looked at the phone's screen but struggled to
focus on the icons, it was instantly coated with a thin
film of rainwater, making it difficult to see the phone.

Rachel stared at the graveyard gates, secured with old
rusted chains, as she wiped the phone on her sweater.
The phone beeped a low battery warning.

'Oh, for fuck's sake!' Rachel shouted and launched a
kick at the gates in frustration. But instead of absorbing

the force of the kick, the chain unravelled, and the gates burst open, making her fall forward.

Caught off guard, she staggered through them trying to stay on her feet but fell to her knees, cutting them on the rough asphalt; her phone clattered on the ground and smashed.

Rachel got up to one knee, 'damn you Kim, where are…' she began to say, but before she could finish her sentence somebody hit her on the back of the head with enough anger that it spun her around viciously.

Rachel hit the ground hard, her left arm whipped around to violently smash into the ground. She tried to see her attacker, but when she moved, pain flooded into her head as if she was being stabbed in the brain by a million needles.

Rachel looked up at the moon, and it looked down at her unsympathetically and then suddenly, its brightness disappeared. Maybe it didn't like what it was about to witness. It took a moment for her to realise that they had pulled a blindfold over her head, a sandbag smelling of dank earth. As the clutches of claustrophobia began to take hold, she sensed somebody near to her. Rachel listened intently, but she couldn't hear anything over the throb in her head. She reached up to pull at the sack, but before she could, she felt hands grab her by the shoulders as she was dragged further into the darkness of the graveyard. Blood oozed from the back of her head, and she felt cold grass, dirt and broken glass cut into her lower back, some of it finding its way inside the back of her skirt but she was too dazed to stop them. She could hear exertion in the breathing, whoever was dragging her was struggling. The dragging stopped, and Rachel sensed that they were kneeling behind her. She felt her shoulder being stroked fondly before a hand clumsily slipped inside her bra. She felt repulsed by their cold hand on the warm skin of her breast. The attacker lingered there for a while. Time seemed to stand; still, Rachel didn't know how long it had been since she'd left the market to find Kim, it could be minutes or hours.

Is this even happening to me?

Am I dreaming?

   Her thoughts were interrupted when her attacker began dragging her again, pulling her limp body over the grass, the heel of her shoe snagged and came off. Her foot cut a trail into the wet earth.

No. It's not a dream… definitely not a dream…

   Finally, they came to rest in a dark corner of the graveyard which smelled of decay, damp rotting leaves and urine.

This is not real…

She felt her skirt being pulled at.

No…

Rachel heard the ripping of fabric at her waist.

Please no, God, please no!

She tried to scream as she felt hands on her thighs, but if she did cry out, nobody heard her. Nobody, not even God himself. The whole of Rachel's body was numb, and she couldn't feel anything. Anything that is except the feeling of her tears as they ran down her cheeks into her hair.

Am I awake?

Dark, it's so dark, why…is…it dark…

Time didn't make sense to her as she drifted in and out of consciousness.

How long have I…?

Kim? Is that…? Are you here… now?

Rachel blinked hard, clearing the dirt and mascara out of her eyes trying to see.

'Who?' she said weakly, her throat was sore when she tried to speak, and the words came out as a pathetic croak. She closed her eyes to fight the pain in her head and passed out.

CHAPTER FIFTY-THREE

From bad to worse

Rachel came to and lay for a while on the ground, waiting to build up enough strength to stand. When she finally made it to her feet, she looked around for her phone and shoe, but it was so dark she couldn't see either of them.

Her left hand had swollen and throbbed with pain, so Rachel cradled it close to her chest with her right hand as she shuffled toward the graveyard gates. She saw her missing shoe on the ground and almost in a trance she slipped her foot into it with barely a pause. The gates were still wide open, and she warily walked towards them, timidly looking around. Her face was a mask of terror with makeup smudged all over her face, and blood from her cut knees running down her legs. If anyone had seen her, they would have paid her little concern, if anything, they would have complimented her on wearing such a good Halloween costume.

Rachel walked along the old cobbled pathway in the centre of the graveyard towards the road in a zig-zagging fashion still unsteady on her feet, severely concussed. Rachel was almost at the entrance but had strayed from the path, stumbling she fell facedown into a mound of dead flowers that the tour guides had removed from the graves. Rachel rolled over onto her back - above her, she could see a face looking down at her.

Doesn't make sense…

This doesn't make any sense; I must be remembering what happened.

Shivering with fear, unable to move or to comprehend what was happening, Rachel just stared back up at the face.

'It's not real, this is not real — you are not real,' Rachel whimpered over and over again, but when the moon finally reappeared, she saw the glint of a needle and recognised the face of the doctor smiling down at her.

CHAPTER FIFTY-FOUR

One

I remember when I was at school. I hated it; I was always in trouble. I guess I couldn't conform to their rules. What was their 'mission statement' again? That's it, via veritas vita. It means 'the way the life' or some shit like that. Follow the way of God's son and everything will work out okay for you. Sure. Until it doesn't. You should never give up hope our teachers used to say in their assemblies. But surely hope is relative to the situation? I'll explain what I mean. When I was young, I had a horse. It belonged to a farmer who had died suddenly, and when his sister, who had inherited his farm turned up, she couldn't wait to get rid of it quickly enough. Couldn't be bothered looking after that when she was busy selling the farm could she now? I loved that damn horse.

No matter how bad things were at home, just spending time with him would always make the world seem right again. One day he seemed off colour and just lay down and wouldn't get up. His big brown eyes, normally full of love, looked dull and sad. He was sick, close to dying the vet said. We'll try this treatment and that treatment. It's not looking good but don't give up hope he had said. All I could do was watch. And hope. Did I pray? I can't remember. But I do know that I never gave up hope. It was so good when he eventually stood up, had a drink and ate a mouthful of grass. Perhaps my faith was repaid, and you know what? He lived for another five years. But in the grand scheme of things, how much does a horse's life matter? Is it worth more or less than a humans? It's all relative, you see. Perhaps my hope was repaid, perhaps not, but I hope that when they find out they understand why I did it. Why I had to kill them, because you see at that time, there was no hope and isn't it all relative in the end anyway?

CHAPTER FIFTY-FIVE

Elephants Don't Float

The car pulled to a stop at the traffic lights and waited, although there was nobody else on the street the doctor didn't want to draw any attention by jumping the lights. The car was one that you wouldn't look twice at, small and bland with the dents and scratches that you would expect. He had chosen it carefully, after all, he had planned well for this moment when he would take revenge on the family of the infidel who had taken everything away from him all those years ago. One of the wing mirrors was missing, and there was a thin crack in the windscreen which stretched almost halfway across it; on a bright sunny day, it caught the light in just the right way to nearly blind the driver.

Today was not one of those sunny days. A fine mist of rain was falling, but the windscreen wipers had not been turned on. The engine was running steadily pumping out its exhaust gases into the chill air as it sat waiting for the traffic lights to change. The hanging lights swayed a little in the slight breeze and eventually changed from red to green. The car still did not move. Minutes passed before the lights changed again from green to amber and then finally to red, but still, the car didn't move.

'Rachel?' the doctor said — his accent drew her name out, making it sound to her like 'Racheel'. She had slumped forward in the seat when the car stopped and stayed in that position as she listened to him.

'Do you know where you are Racheel?' the doctor asked.

When she did not reply, he jabbed at the cut on her temple with his index finger.

'Fuck, yes, I know! Get off me. Berlin, we're on the outskirts of Berlin!' She pushed his hand away, the zip ties that he'd bound her wrists with dug into her skin.

In school, they'd studied the town as an example of the great decline of the American manufacturing industry. Berlin was once a thriving town with hundreds of thousands of people, now it was practically deserted and designated as a place for widespread urban renewal. She had read that the remaining sixty-thousand or so people living here had been given compulsory purchase orders for their properties. Soon after, the steady trickle of people leaving quickly turned into a flood of people fleeing the area looking for their next American Dream. There used to be two thriving paper mills operating here, processing thousands of logs each year.

As Rachel looked down the street to the river at the derelict mills and the water rushing past them, she could almost imagine the massive wooden rafts of logs being ridden by the very men who had felled them upstream. Generations of families had known nothing else but working on the river — now they had gone taking their skills and traditions with them. Rachel knew that even in its heyday, these were not the sort of streets that joggers would pant down. Sighing, Rachel stretched out her arms and put her hands on to the dashboard, causing her sleeves to ride up exposing her wrists. She stared at the fresh cuts and not so new cuts that she had made and wondered if the urge to self-harm would ever leave; her injured hand throbbed as if in response.

'Don't worry Racheel, your pain will soon end. Everything will end.'

Rachel wiped dried blood from her cheek, 'you're crazy, how the hell do you think you will get away with this. Kidnapping or abduction or whatever the hell this is you will get...'

A single long beep of the horn stopped Rachel. She looked around confused at first at where it was coming from until she realised that it was the doctor.

'See,' he said, taking his hand from the steering wheel, 'no one to hear and no one will come. It ends today.'

He saw her looking at the gun resting in his lap, and he shook his head.

'No Racheel, this is not the way, I do not want to shoot you.'

After a moment of uncomfortable silence between them, he yanked the keys from the ignition, motioning with them for her to get out of the car. Rachel opened the door slowly and looked back down the road weighing up her options. Perhaps she could rush the man or just run away, taking her chances against him shooting her in the back. He tapped the top of the car, the metallic rap echoed sadly from the walls of nearby buildings.

'Did your father teach you how to bowl Racheel?

Mine did, they said it was an American tradition Racheel and that it was a father's duty to teach their children American traditions.'

Puzzled, Rachel kicked absently at the tyre of the car, 'what are you talking about? No, no he didn't, he was gone before I was old enough,' she paused, 'he was dead.'

'Ha! Dead! I hated my parents.' He spat onto the ground, then wiped his mouth with the back of his hand.

'But it was his choice Racheel wasn't it?'

She frowned at him and looked over to the hill that the locals called the 'Elephant,' supposedly because it resembled a fat elephant laying on its side.

'In there, we go in there now.'

Rachel saw him looking over her shoulder at an old bowling alley near to where he had stopped the car. Rachel looked at the drab building, painted in a strange shade of green which was probably the same coat of paint used when it had initially opened in the sixties.

The doors and windows were boarded up, and there were large patches of paint flaking and peeling away, exposing bare brickwork in places. The building gave off a sense of despair as she imagined what it would have been like in its glory. Probably had the ribbon cut by a local low-level celebrity or a self-serving politician who saw a photo opportunity. Families would have gathered, with their excitable children ready to gorge themselves on free ice-cream and fizzy soda as they watched their fathers trying to beat their workmates.

But that was long ago, and the building that was once filled with joy and laughter now stood empty. If it was possible for an inanimate object to look depressed, then this was what it would look like. The thick wooden boards looked like they'd been nailed in place years ago and Rachel saw that even they had begun to rot away in places and then she noticed the dull grey metal chain and heavy padlock threaded through a hole in each door.

'Open it,' was all he said, as he tossed a key towards Rachel's feet.

She fished them out from the weeds growing out of a crack in the sidewalk, and when she turned to him, he looked different, something about his manner had changed. Some layer of control had slipped, and Rachel was unsure whether he was nervous or excited or both but what she was sure of was that she would never leave this place alive.

She looked around, careful to avoid his stare, sensing his impatience as she heard his shoes scuff the road as he kicked at a crumpled tin can.

Rachel slid the key into the lock and paused to take in the surroundings, she saw the decline, the rotting disused buildings, and as she heard the lock click open, she turned and saw the Elephant.

Stupid Elephant — you probably came here to die like everything else in this shit hole she thought.

CHAPTER FIFTY-SIX
Reunion

The doctor locked the door to the street behind them and pushed her towards a door to the right. Rachel stumbled into the room and looked around. It was almost dark apart from the dull green light coming from hospital machines surrounding a man who lay on the hospital bed.

In one corner was a long wooden box with the hospital's name, some kind of serial code and phone number painted on its side. Confused, Rachel turned to look at the doctor before looking back at the man on the bed.

'Who is this?' She asked.

The doctor let out a thin wheezy laugh which turned into a raspy cough.

He thumped his chest to clear his throat before saying, 'you do not recognise — this man?' Pointing to the man in the bed.

'Who the hell is he? What are you doing here?'

Rachel watched as the man's chest rose and fell in time with the ventilator that was supplying him with oxygen and Kyles face appeared before her eyes, slowing falling into a deep sleep that he would never wake up from. The doctor coughed, snapping her back to the present then he jabbed her in the back with the end of the pistol.

'Look closer, look at his face.'

Her anger built, but after a moment, she moved nearer to the bed and leaned in closer to stare at his face.

'Who is he? What's he got to do with me?'

'Ha! What has he got to do with you? You ask the wrong questions, Racheel, you should ask what he has to do with me!'

Wringing his hands together as if dry washing them, he added impatiently, 'well, go on then, ask!'

Rachel shrugged, 'okay, what's he done to you?'

He took in a deep breath and held it for a second, the moment he had thought about for years now upon him.

'Done to me, he has taken everything from me. Everything,' he paused, then repeated, 'everything,' so quietly that Rachel could just about hear him over the hiss of the ventilator.

Rachel felt the sharp edges of the plastic zip ties dig into her wrists, and she pressed harder against them relishing the dull throbbing feeling. It had been so many years since she'd seen him, but there was something that she recognised, the shape of his eyes maybe. She looked at his hands, but she couldn't see them under the filthy sheet covering him.

'Is he…?'

The doctor's eyes lit up as he urged her to go on.

Rachel turned to the doctor.

'Is it him, is he my father?'

'Yes, that's him. Father!' he spat the words out.

'You disrespect the very word by calling him that. Your father is nothing more than a filthy pig — you should be ashamed of him.'

She stood up too quickly and feeling dizzy she staggered back from the bed, her legs feeling weak beneath her. The doctor saw her swaying and put the gun down on to the table by the door. He grabbed her roughly by the shoulders and directed her to the long, rough wooden box in the corner of the room. She put her hands between her legs to shift position and felt thin splinters of wood penetrate her palms. As she moved her hands away from the sharp points, her fingers found a circular hole drilled into the side of the box. Rachel felt around and found several more in seemingly random positions as if they'd been hurriedly cut out.

'So why are you doing this, is he even really alive? Is this why you did this to my mother, why are you punishing our family?'

'Him, that's why. All because of him,' the doctor pointed to the man on the bed.

'He took away my family. Now I take away yours,' he added with a hint of sadness in his voice which Rachel thought was odd in the circumstances.

'You tried once remember? I got my mother away from you, and the police will catch up with you, and when they do, you will be going away for a very long time. Or maybe they'll give you the death penalty, that's what you deserve.'

He shrugged his shoulders.

'No matter, I do not fear death as you American's do. For a nation that causes so much death to others around the world, I find it shameful that you still fear it.'

Rachel dug her nails into the wood.

Keep him talking, that way, maybe Kim will notice I haven't made it home before he tries to hurt me.

'They'll come soon to save me, you know, the Police or my friends you'll see.'

He let out a trill laugh that deteriorated into another long coughing fit. Rachel found herself feeling embarrassed for him for some reason.

'Friends? You mean, Kim?' He began laughing again, fighting off another cough.

'I was coming to kill you all in your sleep, you know. We waited outside your house… '

'Hang on, what are you talking about we, who the hell is we?'

He smiled at her, a thin-lipped knife slash of a smile.

'Kyle, the pervert I caught messing in women's underwear when they were in the operating theatre. I groomed him further of course, and then when he started messing with unconscious women, I knew I had him. I set up a room in the hospital basement and recorded what he was doing to them. The weak fool broke down in tears when I started blackmailing him to help me, he even admitted touching the dead ones as well. I didn't know about that at first, but after he told me that he had no way out.'

'Fuck.'

'Yes, fuck indeed,' he replied and smiled again when he saw her body sag.

'We were about to come in, and we saw that so-called friend of yours, Kim jogging up and then she crawled under your mother's car and did something. So, we waited all night.'

'The oil leak? Kim always said she would make my mother pay for hurting me, but I never thought...' she said quietly.

'The next day we followed the car. It was hard to see with all the snow; it sometimes snows in Kurdistan too you know. And then we rammed it, making it swerve off the road into the water. And let me tell you the water was cold, Racheel, freezing cold.'

Rachel stared at him, 'You! You were the off duty doctor that saved her?'

His eyes grew wide with excitement, 'yes, it was perfect Racheel. The pervert went back with the ambulance and made sure my name did not show up in the medical report and another pervert pig friend of his altered the records to remove my work history. I became, how do you say it - a ghost.'

Rachel thought back to when she had seen Kyle at the hospital and remembered the porter pushing the young girl down the corridor.

'The porter?' She asked. 'Did he change your records?'

He laughed, 'him! No, that stupid fool was only good for pushing people around and cleaning up shit but when I threatened to tell his wife he had been touching children he convinced his receptionist slut mistress to do it.'

Rachel felt a numbness flow through her.
She nodded towards the whiteboard above the bed, 'what does that mean, 49? Is it part of a medical number or something?' She asked before turning back to him.

'Don't worry about that. Now for your sake, I want you to stay very still,' he said as he walked towards her with a needle.

CHAPTER FIFTY-SEVEN

Numbers

'Stay very still,' he said as he walked towards her with a needle and surgical thread. Images of Kyle's lifeless body flooded her thoughts, and Rachel pulled her head out of the way.

'What, so if you are going to kill me, why bother stitching me up?'

He held her chin to keep her head still as he dabbed away at the cut on her head with an alcohol wipe. He had a look of indignation on his face.

'I am a professional, I intend to do a professional job, so the final image that I see will be your perfect deaths.'

She looked into his eyes as he worked on her face and could hear a slight wheeze on his chest as he breathed in. He held up a syringe in front of her face, and she shook her head.

'No? It is simply pain relief; it will take away the pain when I stitch.'

'No needles,' Rachel tensed until she saw him place the needle back onto the table.

'Very well,' he said, as he began to stitch Rachel's face.

Tears ran down her cheeks as she felt her skin being pierced and pulled at, but she was surprised at how quickly he finished. When she opened her eyes, he nodded in satisfaction at his work.

'So, you are a real doctor?'

He looked affronted, 'of course! When I came to this country, my adoptive parents made sure that I got excellent grades at school and then paid for me to study at the finest medical schools.'

'When did you come to this country?' Rachel asked.

He looked puzzled, 'when the soldiers found me, of course, after he killed them all. The men, the women, the children — all of them. You must be very proud of him.'

Rachel ignored his taunt as she looked around the room for a way out, but the only way out was past him. She saw the silver gun on the table. Rachel fidgeted on the box. Maybe she could reach it.

'They took everything, even my name. They found a blanket with the name "Ayden" on it next to a dead baby, so they just called me Aiden Massy after the valley they found me in.'

'Kani Masi,' Rachel said dully, turning to look at him.

He met her gaze, 'yes, everybody dead, poisoned with your fake weapons of mass destruction.' He coughed into his hand and wiped it on his sleeve.

'Some soldiers saved me, found me hidden,

surrounded by dead people. Sent me to an aid station before I was brought here as a refugee, I went into the care system and eventually, some sterile old people took me in. I used them well, acting like the grateful son for them. One day when they thought I was old enough to understand, they gave me a dog-tag that they said was found near to my home in Iraq, and that's how I found him.'

Rachel looked at the number written on the whiteboard above the man in the bed. 'You tracked him down from a dog-tag?'

He let out a small odd laugh, 'my American parents did it actually, but it turned out that it wasn't your father's details on the dog-tag. It was by luck too. The old fools used the Online Military Database, but they typed the number wrong — they weren't your fathers they belonged to some other soldier who had the same number as your father, well the same except for the last one. As soon as I had his name, I found the veterans care home your country had rewarded him with, created some fake transfer documents took him to that house before bringing him here. Then, from that, I used his medical records to track down his next of kin and tracked you down in Boston.

'What happened to them, your American parents?'

The doctor shrugged, 'oh them, they died. Once they were of no use to me, I took their lives. I was very careful Racheel. One day when the old man was out, I made his stupid slut of a wife swallow her tongue. No evidence you see.'

Rachel touched the stitches on the side of her head and glanced at the gun on the table, if he saw her look, he made no comment and continued with his story.

'The old man was so devastated that he took many pills and fell asleep next to her. A beautiful story, no?'

'So what?' Rachel said, 'you're going to kill us, is that your plan?'

'Oh yes, you will all die today, and I will make sure that it is you who will take the blame. You have been keeping him here hoping that he will wake up, but when he didn't you were so ashamed of his war crimes and couldn't bear the truth coming out, and you ended it like the cowards' you people are. How does that sound?'

Rachel looked at him, 'You won't get away with it. The police are already looking for you and when Kim realises I'm missing she'll go to them as well.'

His face held an expression she couldn't quite read, confusion perhaps.

He shook his head, 'Kim? She was the one who attacked you in the graveyard, you should thank me for stopping her.'

Rachel looked at him blankly, 'what do you mean?' She said slowly.

He shrugged his shoulders then pointed to the man on the hospital bed, 'he ruined your future because of what he did in his past.'

Rachel stood up and walked over to the bed and leaned in close to study his face looking for any sign that he could hear her, understand what was happening. The glow from the machines next to him caught his face casting strange shadows in the hollows of his cheeks.

'498 dash 4576,' the doctor said.

Rachel watched the man's chest rise and fall, 'what?'

'His service number, I memorised it of course 498 dash 4576, the number of your murdering pig of a father.'

Rachel looked at the drip coming from his hand and traced its path towards the stand that held the sagging bag of saline. The room was uncomfortably quiet except for the click and hiss of the ventilator. Rachel stared at the small whiteboard above his head. Something wasn't right. She looked at the saline bag again and traced its path back towards his hand under the sheet, the clear tube hung down at the side of the bed, and as Rachel looked at it, she realised what was missing. There were no bags to collect his urine, either he was dead already, or he would be soon.

She turned to look at the doctor, he was still standing with his back to the door, when she looked into his eyes, she saw a hardness there, and his hand-wringing stopped. Rachel knew it would be over soon. The gun was still on the table, but he held a large needle in his hand, a different one than before, longer and thicker. He shook his head slowly when he saw her look past him at the gun.

But it wasn't the gun she was looking at; she was looking at the door which slowly opened to reveal a silhouetted figure.

CHAPTER FIFTY-EIGHT
Waiting Room

There were toys scattered all over the floor. Dog-eared books with ripped and missing pages, cars with wonky wheels, everything in the sort of condition that you would find in a doctor's waiting room. Children would play with them not really caring about breaking or getting them dirty because they didn't belong to them, they had newer, more expensive toys at home. The doctor would call them in, and the children just dropped the toys where they were to dutifully trot in after their parents and watch as they nodded at what the doctor would tell them before they left with a slip of paper which was then swapped for pills.

He was restless today and cold, the thick radiators were like blocks of ice when he touched them. The man had not come back last night to bring him food, and as he read the side of an empty candy bar wrapper, he felt his stomach rumble. Maybe the man would bring him hot food today, perhaps a burger and some fries and if he was lucky maybe a comic book as well because he had been a good boy. It was important to be a good boy, so he kept his room tidy, went to the toilet when he was told to, although the bucket smelled, and even washed in one of the sinks in the bathroom. Never once complaining that the water was cold - he hated cold water, especially after that day, but he never told the man that.

He didn't know exactly how long he'd been in the room, but his hair had grown longer, and if he pulled on it, it nearly touched his shoulders.

He had heard him through the door once smashing things up and cursing. He had heard people swear before and knew lots of the words that people shouldn't use, but he didn't recognise some of them. Even his mother had not used them, and she was very good at cursing. He stared at the small window set high in the wall and guessed that it was at least early afternoon as the streetlight outside had not come on yet.

He liked the yellow light when it came on at night because he could still see when the strip lights in his room were turned off by the man. There were lots of flies in the light covering, and he thought that you must be sort of dumb to let yourself become trapped like that.

He wrapped a blanket around his shoulders as he paced the room, he didn't really mind how it scratched his skin anymore - he had gotten used to that now.

He tried the doorknob not really expecting it to open, but it had become a habit now. As long as he had been here, wherever here was, the man always locked the door when he left. As he rested his hand on the cold metal handle, he paused. The handle creaked as the old springs inside the mechanism were compressed, and he pulled.

This time it opened, and Josh walked through.

It was dark in the old bowling alley, but Josh had spent months in the dark and is eyes adjusted quickly to the gloom. A green exit sign flickered and drew Josh towards the door leading out to the road. He tried the handle, turning it carefully - maybe it was his lucky day, and it would open.

The handle turned and clicked, but it had been locked by the doctor when he had come back. Tears welled up in Josh's eyes, but he fought them away; he wasn't a baby anymore, and he didn't want the man to see him crying.

Josh turned to go back to his room, and that was when he saw the door to another room. People were talking in there; he could hear a man and a woman's voice. It sounded familiar.

CHAPTER FIFTY-NINE

Luck

Josh pushed the door open slowly. Despite the creaking noise it made, the doctor seemed unaware until he saw Rachel's eyes grow wide with surprise as she saw her brother for the first time in months.

'Josh?' She said, walking towards him.

The doctor held his arm out in front of her. 'No - you sit down, stay where you are.' Then he turned to face Josh.

Josh held the gun with two hands, but even so, his arms were shaking with the weight of it. Months of malnutrition had left him so weak.

'Josh? How are...' Rachel began to ask.

The doctor cut her off mid-sentence to answer the question he knew she was asking, 'laryngospasm - near-drowning. His throat closed instinctively in the cold water. He was lucky I was there.'

'Lucky!' Rachel spat out the words, 'this is all because of you!'

Tears ran down her face when she looked at Josh. His beautiful curls were gone, and his hair hung lank and greasy around his shoulders. She looked him up and down, he was wearing baggy trousers and an oversized woolly sweater with food stains down the front. On his feet, he wore a pair of black and white bowling shoes which were two sizes too big, making him look like he was trying to dress like a neglected clown. Rachel could smell how unclean he was from the other side of the room.

Josh opened his mouth to speak but said nothing. Tears ran down his face, carving streaks through the dirt on his cheeks. The doctor rushed at him, closing the distance between them surprisingly quickly, lunging at the gun as he tried to pin Josh against the door. Josh's ribs cracked and he let out a silent gasp as he felt one tear through his skin and snag on the woollen sweater. The doctor grabbed for the barrel, and as he slammed Josh into the door, the gun went off. The bullet tore through the flesh of the doctor's palm, before slamming into the wall.

Josh cried out in pain as his finger caught and broke in the trigger guard as the doctor yanked the gun away from him.

As soon as the doctor had launched himself at Josh, Rachel was on her feet. As the doctor grabbed at the gun Josh held, she jumped onto the man's back, wrapping her arms around his throat. The plastic ties holding her hands together cut into the skin of his neck. He stumbled forward, then one of his knees gave out on him, and they fell backwards, crashing into the bed. Rachel pulled harder, but the ties snapped, and the gun skidded over the floor in a circular motion before coming to rest next

to the wooden crate she had been sitting on only
moments ago.

Rachel saw stars as she hit her head on the metal bed
frame and released the grip on his neck. It took her a
moment to realise where she was as she looked up at the
flaking paint and black mould on the ceiling.

Something thick and warm dripped down her neck,
and when she dabbed at it and looked at her fingers, she
knew instantly that it was blood. Rachel felt the stitches
on her face, but they were still intact, maybe it was the
doctor's blood. She heard him let out a groan and
muttered and insult as he staggered to his feet and
picked up the gun. The blood on his hands made it hard
to grip, and he fumbled with it. Rachel heard a metallic
sound as he dropped the gun. She watched him pick it up
carefully and walk over to her.

This is it Rachel thought as he stood over her and
pointed the gun at her head. Blood dripped onto the floor
from his injured hand, and he wiped it against his trouser
leg. His eyes narrowed as he looked down the top of the
pistol and lined up the front and rear sights. Rachel saw
his arm straighten slightly as he took up the first trigger
pressure. She closed her eyes, waiting for her life to
end, wondering what it would be like to die.

CHAPTER SIXTY

Fault Lines

He kicked her foot. 'Open your eyes. Watch as I first take your brother's life.'

Rachel looked past the doctor at Josh, who was curled up in a ball whimpering as he held his chest. He was taking deep breaths which made a strange wet sucking noise which made her feel sick. The doctor kicked her again then turned, pointed the gun at Josh, and pulled the trigger.

Nothing happened.

The safety catch had been knocked into the safe position when the gun had slid across the floor. The doctor tilted the gun to look at it; then he pushed the safety lever to the fire position and raised the gun again, taking up the first trigger pressure.

Rachel grabbed the frame of the bed, hauling herself to her feet. She saw him looking down the sights of the pistol and looked around frantically for something to hit him with.

There was nothing.

She pulled the plastic tube of the saline drip from the man's hand and ran at the doctor, wrapping the tube around his neck. She put her knee into the small of his back and pulled as hard as she could until they fell over onto their sides. The plastic dug into the skin of the doctors neck and found purchase in his trachea just below his Adam's apple.

He dropped the gun and clawed at Rachels face and eyes. She felt sharp fingernails scratch her eyes and a finger jabbed her pupil, making her see double. Rachel turned her head sideways and pressed her forehead into the base of his skull.

His legs thrashed around, and his shins banged against the legs of the bed as he tried to squirm away, but she wrapped her legs around him as she continued to strangle him.

Rachel felt the plastic tubing stretch. The doctor no longer clawed at her face. He pulled at her hands, trying to prise her fingers apart, but he couldn't release her grip.

And then the plastic tube snapped.

The doctor gulped in air and tried to get up. Rachel grabbed hold of his ear pulling roughly so that his head faced the ceiling and with the other hand she stabbed the two-inch cannula into his right eye, pushing until she felt her thumb touch his eyeball. His legs twitched as Rachel moved the cannula from side to side in his eye socket.

His body stiffened momentarily before sagging limp and lifeless on top of her.

She shoved him off of her, spat into his face and crawled over to Josh, pulling him into her arms.

'Did I do good Rach — with the gun?' he whispered, clearly in a lot of pain. She looked at the machine next to the bed, the steady peaks and troughs became erratic as the man's heart rate rose and fell quickly.

'You did great Joshy, really good, I'm so proud of you.

Rachel saw that the man was bleeding from his side, a pool of blood had formed under the bed. She could see the shattered plaster on the far wall where the bullet had become lodged after passing through his stomach.

'Rachel, who is that man? The one on the bed?'

Rachel looked at his hand, hanging over the edge to the bed, part of his little finger was missing. Father, war hero, war criminal - Rachel made a snap decision to protect Josh from the truth, he'd been through so much already.

'Him? He's nobody.'

The green line became straight as the man on the bed died. Rachel made no attempt so save him and watched as his life drifted away.

Finally, she looked at Josh and said, 'come on, we need to find Kim, she's got some explaining to do.'

CHAPTER SIXTY-ONE

Zero

Like most people who have been murdered, I knew my killer. I didn't die by a random act of violence committed by a stranger, in fact, I knew them very well.

Epilogue

Next of Kin

Kim could hear the shouting and noise of a gun going off.

She screamed over and over again, but the gag in her mouth stole the sound, and she had to stop in case she threw up and suffocated in her own vomit.

She could hear Rachels voice. The last time she had heard it was in the graveyard when she was teaching her a lesson for ignoring her and fooling around with Steve. All Kim wanted was to rough her up a bit, take some compromising photos, and then Rachel would have to be with her. It was going so well until something had stung her neck and the next thing she knew she had woken up in this box. This box, like some sort of coffin.

They were arguing, Rachel and the doctor, but there was another voice, a boy.

No, it can't be! She strained her neck to see out of the holes but saw only shadows as people moved around, fighting and screaming at each other.

Kim wanted to kick out or hit the side of the box to let Rachel know she was inside it, but she couldn't. She pushed against the bottom of the box and tried to kick out, but her bare toes could only brush against the wood. Her hands and legs were bound tight, there was not enough room to move, and when she tried to, her legs began to cramp up. The rough wood made her naked shoulder blades hurt.

There was a final clattering of metal and then silence. Kim waited for Rachel to open to the box and let her out, but Kim only heard doors banging shut and something which sounded like the rattle of a chain being pulled and the faint click of a padlock.

Kim waited, alone, frightened.

And then she screamed, a terrible, silent scream that nobody ever heard.

Scott Barron

Printed in Great Britain
by Amazon